ROSEMO
HIMSELF

In the dim light of dawn, indistinct figures raced toward him, their weapons firing. He rolled behind his empty recon capsule and zeroed in on them. Now that he could use his LAR's laser sight, he switched the rifle over to the three-round burst mode.

His first burst took the lead hostile in the chest. Triggering off two more short bursts, he sent two more men to the ground, and the others broke off and raced for cover. Checking his tac display, Rosemont saw the locator beacons of Strider Charlie over to his left. Flashing his intentions, he quickly joined up with the team as they got busy clearing out the scattered pockets of hostiles.

Silence finally fell over the airfield, broken only by the crackling flames from the burning hangars. Several Peacekeepers were fighting the fire, mainly to keep the column of smoke from announcing their presence.

Not that their airborne landing could be kept a secret. So much for secrecy and Force Intel's information about what they were facing.

This had not been a good way to start the day.

Also available in this series:
WARKEEP 2030

KILLING FIELDS

Michael Kasner

TORONTO • NEW YORK • LONDON
AMSTERDAM • PARIS • SYDNEY • HAMBURG
STOCKHOLM • ATHENS • TOKYO • MILAN
MADRID • WARSAW • BUDAPEST • AUCKLAND

First edition March 1993

ISBN 0-373-62015-2

KILLING FIELDS

Printed in U.S.A.

KILLING FIELDS

1

Johannesburg, August 9, 2030

From a distance Johannesburg looked almost the same as it had back in the late 1990s. Once inside the city, however, anyone who had known Jo'burg when it had been the financial center of the nation then known as the Republic of South Africa would instantly see that it was not really the same place at all. In the year 2030, the city was a bare skeleton of its former self.

As had happened fifty years before in neighboring Zimbabwe, the transition from white minority rule in South Africa to a black majority government in 2008 had gone more or less peacefully at first. Again following the pattern set by Zimbabwe, the dream of the two races living in peace and harmony evaporated immediately after the first universal election.

During the final days of white rule, there had been only three major Black political parties: the African National Congress, the Zulu Inkatha Freedom Party and the radical People's Democratic Movement. Once the blacks assumed power, however, suddenly there were dozens of rival factions vying to rule, and their discussions were conducted with firearms. When the shooting finally ended, an all-black government was formed from a coalition of several of the more radical factions.

The first thing the new government did was to rename the country the Bantu People's Democracy. The new government didn't label itself Marxist, but as the name indicated, it was. This brand of Marxism had nothing to do with giving to "each according to his needs." Like the Marxist states of the previous century, this government was only interested in giving to those in power according to their desires. The rest of the population could shift for themselves.

After renaming the nation, the coalition partners immediately renewed their fighting, and what remained of the once prosperous nation began a long slide into economic decline.

Despite all this, there was still a considerable white population in the country. Many of them had stayed because they still held to the ideal that they could live in harmony and prosper under the new black government. Others had been forced to stay when the government, fearing a "brain drain," closed the borders.

Both blacks and whites suffered over the next twenty years as the factional fighting continued unabated. As soon as one political party was eliminated, another rose in its place and the fighting continued. The last hope for both the whites and the blacks was John Bolothu, the moderate leader of the new Centrist Party, which had captured the national election of 2029. Six months after the election, it looked as if the Centrist Party was slowly bringing peace to the nation.

President Bolothu was in Johannesburg to install the newly elected Centrist mayor of the city. In an unusual gesture of solidarity, his political rival and vice president, the fiery Madame Jewel Jumal, stood at his side. The main obstacle to Bolothu's bringing a permanent peace to his nation was that he had been forced to form a political alliance with Jumal's radical People's Democratic Movement.

More than once, Jumal had pledged that she would do everything in her power to finish purging the remaining white population from the Bantu People's Democracy. Bolothu, however, saw the whites as an important, integral part of the nation. Though she and the president often clashed over their political philosophies, her appearance on the same podium with him on this occasion was seen as a hopeful sign.

ON A THREE-STORY ROOFTOP across from the People's Square in Johannesburg, a muscular black man knelt behind the balustrade and opened a battered suitcase. Inside the suitcase lay an Argentine-made 8 mm semiautomatic sniper rifle fitted with a 20-power autoranging scope and a silencer. Firing EHE—Enhanced High Explosive—tipped ammunition, the rifle could reach to well over 1500 meters. The speaker's platform on the far side of the square below was no farther then five hundred.

When President Bolothu stepped up to the microphone, the sniper raised his rifle and focused the autoranging scope on the center of Bolothu's chest. When the stadia marks lined up on the man's head and feet and the vertical line bisected his body, the sniper took a deep breath. Letting the air out slowly, he triggered the silenced rifle.

The first round hit the president in the center of his rib cage, and there was no need for a second shot. The enhanced high-explosive pellet in the core of the bullet blew Bolothu's upper body apart. Blood and tissue spattered the other dignitaries on the speaker's stand as they dived for cover. When the sound of the exploding round echoed away, only Madame Jumal still stood, blood dripping from her clothes and a secret smile on her face.

ACROSS THE BORDER in the neighboring country of Mozambique, a thousand armed and uniformed men waited in a staging area. These men were all white and they spoke Afrikaans, the language of the Boers who had fled South Africa when the white majority government fell in 2008. The leader of this well-armed strike force was Jan Rikermann, the charismatic leader of the Boer government in exile. The United Nations did not recognize his government's existence, but that was of no concern to Rikermann. The thousand men he led did recognize him as their leader and they would soon be followed by several thousand more.

A slow, seldom-seen smile cut across Rikermann's face as the Boer leader read the printout in his hands. Just as his Intelligence agents in Pretoria had predicted, Madame Jumal had successfully assassinated President Bolothu and now was loudly blaming the whites in Johannesburg for his death. Jumal had ordered her Simba political troops to incarcerate all the white citizens in the country until they could be put on trial for the assassination. Now the world would see that the black government was totally corrupt and had to be overthrown.

"We are ready, Dov," he said to the short, dark, wiry man standing at the other end of the room. "Praise God, we are finally ready. We cross the border this afternoon."

Dov Merov also smiled. The Israeli weapons engineer was pleased because not only would the new South Africa be the Boer homeland, but it would also be the homeland for the thousands of his countrymen who had grown weary of living in the religiously oppressive Jewish state of Israel.

Starting in 1990, Israel had been flooded with Russian immigrants. The flood quickly became a torrent as the Jews fled collapsing economies and ethnic violence. By the year 2000, there were virtually no Jews still living in what had been the Soviet Union and the Communist nations of Eastern Europe.

Absorbing this influx had been difficult for Israel. The immigrants brought with them only the barest traces of the traditional Jewish religious practices. This brought them into immediate conflict with the powerful Orthodox religious element in Israeli politics. The new immigrants had come to Israel for the freedom that had long been denied them and a chance to start their lives anew. Bowing their heads to what they saw as superstitious nonsense was not in their plans.

After the abortive Arab-Israeli war of 2004, the ultraconservative Orthodox party took control of the government. They proclaimed that the devastation of the one nuclear weapon that had detonated near Tel Aviv was the judgment of an angry God on a people who had strayed far from His ancient teachings. When they took control, they imposed the old ways by force.

Once a thriving, modern industrial nation, the Israel of 2030 wasn't too different from her Islamic fundamentalist neighbors. Scientific research had been severely curtailed, business hours were strictly regulated, libraries had been purged of "unclean" reading materials and all aspects of private life were rigidly controlled. The Sabras, the nonreligious, native-born Israelis, and the non-Orthodox Jews had virtually no voice in running the government. In the Israel of 2030, Orthodox religious practices ruled supreme.

In the new South Africa Rikermann envisioned, however, the Israelis could live productive lives without having to bend their knees to a rigid religion few of them believed in anymore. That Israelis seeking to escape religious persecution should have teamed up with fanatic Christian Boers who thought they were carrying out God's plan on earth was a fine irony. But it was one that had been born out of desperation.

The time was long past when large numbers of people could relocate to another nation and start over. Merov's own ancestors had come out of Russia fifty years before, but there was no developed nation on earth that would welcome Merov today. The industrial nations had finally learned that allowing unlimited immigration was one of the most destructive things they could do to themselves. Limiting immigration to only those few people they actually needed was absolutely essential if that nation was to continue to exist.

The only place on earth left for the Jews to go was someplace they could create for themselves, and that someplace would be the new South Africa.

"Just think, Dov," Rikermann said, his eyes glittering. "In a few short days, we will have our homeland back. It has been a long struggle, but now it is over."

"What about the Peacekeepers?"

Rikermann snorted. "The arrogant Americans who are always trying to impose their 'order' on the world, what about them? Where were they when the Kaffirs drove our people from their lands? If they are so concerned about injustice, why didn't they try to save us then? They didn't get involved then and they won't do anything now."

He shrugged. "But if they do get in the way, it will make no difference. We are strong now, and well armed, and we will fight them if we have to. No matter what, South Africa will be free again."

Dov Merov had reservations about the Peacekeepers, but he allowed himself to be convinced by the Boer leader because he had to. If his people were to escape persecution and start new lives, Rikermann's operation had to be successful. And for it to be successful, the warheads he had designed for the Boer's missiles would have to fly true.

THE WORLD OF 2030 was somewhat more peaceful than it had been over the past forty years, but what peace there was had been imposed by force of arms. During the great disarmament of the late nineties, the United Nations had tried to control the spread of nuclear-weapons technology, but they failed. They had called upon nations to disarm themselves in the name of peace, brotherhood and civilization, but not everyone answered the call. The United States, the Russian Union of Democratic Republics and the EuroCombine gave up their nukes, but too many nations of the world had refused. Nukes were the best chance for small nations to even old scores, and they wouldn't willingly give them up.

Then came the short Arab-Israeli nuclear exchange of 2004. The strike against Tel Aviv had been launched by a mentally unbalanced Syrian major with hashish-inspired dreams of jihad. The rest of the one-day nuclear war had been conducted by the Israelis. Their missiles had been aimed at military rather than civilian targets, but the destruction had been devastating nonetheless.

The great powers reacted instantly. Led by the United States and the Russians, military strike forces went in and forcefully removed the remaining nuclear weapons from the warring nations. When this operation was over, the major powers then forcefully eliminated the nuclear stockpiles of the rest of the world. Following that, they destroyed the rest of their own nuclear arsenals except for a few held in reserve for use against anyone who decided to start the nuclear arms race again.

Although nuclear weapons had been banned, the knowledge to make them was in the hands of every government on the planet. Since the UN couldn't be trusted to prevent the reproliferation of the banned weapons, a completely new force was needed to undertake this heavy responsibility. The politicians had clearly failed, and now it was time to give the professional soldiers a chance.

In 2006 a joint declaration of the Russian and American governments announced that they would form a new world police force, the Russian and United States expeditionary forces, the Peacekeepers. Drawn from the elite military units of both nations, these troops were the elite of the elite and were equipped with the best weapons and equipment that twenty-first-century technology could produce.

In the international politics of the twenty-first century, no one denied the right of a nation to slaughter its own people or to make limited war along its borders. Warfare has always been mankind's favorite blood sport, and this hadn't changed. Most of these were little wars, however, local affairs more on the order of a soccer match with live ammunition.

But even in this era of military and political realism, wars of conquest were still frowned upon. When armies crossed established national boundaries intent upon destroying their neighbors, they would find the Peacekeepers standing in their path. When the United States Expeditionary Force, or USEF, was sent in, it didn't waste time talking. When the battle was over and the bodies had been counted, the Peacekeepers didn't negotiate a peace settlement; they imposed it.

2

Fort Benning, August 11

United States Expeditionary Force Staff Sergeant Katrina "Kat" Wallenska was in her element. The stocky, dark-haired, green-eyed Echo Company recon grunt was stripped down to fatigue pants and a sweat-soaked T-shirt that clung to her full breasts as if it had been painted on her. A small, sterling-silver skull earring glittered from her right earlobe, and a dull black fighting knife was poised in her hand. Lying at her feet in the sawdust of the training arena was a man wearing fatigue pants and a thin armor training vest over his T-shirt. Kat knelt at his side, the point of her knife pricking the skin of his neck over his carotid artery. The man was keeping very still.

"Listen up, malfs," Wallenska snapped. "This ain't the Regular fucking Army—you're Peacekeepers now. If you want to live long enough to impress the boys and girls back home with your pretty little green berets, you'd better get your RA heads out of your RA asses and pay attention. You come up against a hostile with a knife in his hand, he's not going to give you time to get your head outta your ass. He's gonna kill ya."

Even though the fighting knife in her hand today was reinforced Teflon, Kat Wallenska was the Peacekeepers' foremost exponent of the fine art of cold steel and she was doing one of her favorite things this morning. She was teaching an audience of newly assigned Peacekeepers how to do it unto others before it was done unto them. The trainee facedown in the sawdust, however, hadn't learned the lesson yet.

A tall, muscular black standing in the semicircle of trainees around Kat leaned over to his partner and whispered something in his ear. The other man laughed and looked over at her.

"Yo! Malf!" Kat glared at the first trainee. "You got something to say, you say it so we can all hear it. Out with it."

The trainee smiled insolently and shrugged. "I jus' asked him what time it was, Sarge."

Kat smiled back at him, but there was no humor in her smile. It was the smile of the cat that was just about to eat the canary. "Okay, big man," she said, releasing the victim at her feet and standing up. "Get your ass out here and show me what you've learned today."

The trainee sauntered out into the arena, the knife in his right hand held low at his side. The man was almost a foot taller than the stocky sergeant and had more than fifty pounds on her, but as she intended to show him, knife fighting had nothing to do with size or strength.

As he approached her, he crouched and smoothly shifted the knife to his left hand and then back to his right. Kat took full notice of his fancy knife work and the low, crouching street fighter's stance, both the hallmarks of urban gangs. Considering the trash that the Regular Army enlisted to meet its quota, this guy probably had a criminal record a mile long. He sure as hell had done some street fighting and undoubtedly had knifed someone before. But killing an unarmed citizen, or killing in a street fight, was a far cry from facing off against someone who really knew the art of the blade.

"Okay, bitch," the trainee said softly. "You wanna know what I learned? I learned I'm gonna cut yo tits off."

Wallenska smiled to herself as she faced her opponent. The man's sneering comment had been designed to make her angry and to make her react in anger. It was a typical street fighter's ploy, but it wasn't going to work today. Kat never did anything in the heat of anger. She was the daughter of Polish immigrants, and she hadn't gotten where she was in the world's most elite military unit by being quick-tempered.

But that didn't mean that she took any shit from anybody, either. All it meant was that she picked her own time and place to kick someone's ass whenever he or she needed it. And since this guy was begging for it today, this was a good time and the right place. She'd be happy to give him what he was asking for.

The trainee continued shifting the knife from one hand to the other, trying to draw her eyes down to the movement of the blade. But that, too, was an old trick, and she watched his face instead. A sudden flicker in his eyes telegraphed his move as he suddenly lashed out for her lower belly.

Kat had been expecting the attack and ducked back from the slash. As the blade flashed through empty air in front of her, she stepped back into her opponent. Pivoting slightly to one side, she lashed out with a side kick aimed at his crotch. Though the trainee was wearing a groin protector, Kat's combat boot landed squarely and drove the plastic cup into his testicles with stunning force.

The knife flew from the man's hand, and he doubled over on his way to the ground. As he lay curled up on the sawdust, moaning and clutching his testicles, Kat carefully stepped around him and faced her trainees again. Her face wore a tight smile. "As you just saw, knife fighting can be combined with other forms of combat. The purpose of the exercise is to kill the fucker, not get involved in some fucking dance with him."

She surveyed her audience. "Now, pair off and try some of this."

Kat walked up to the trainee who had laughed at whatever her defeated opponent had said to him. "You and me, malf—" she pointed her knife at him as if it were her index finger "—we're gonna party."

The man took a deep breath. "Yo, Sergeant."

"Get your ass out here, boy."

IN A LOW BRICK BUILDING in the Harmony Church area of Fort Benning, USEF Major Alexander F. Rosemont was sitting in his office in the Echo Company orderly room going through his ration of paperwork for the day. Rosemont was blond and blue-eyed like his namesake, Alexander the Great, but that was where the similarity ended. The legendary Macedonian king had been a small, wiry man, but Rosemont was tall and muscular. In the age of Alexander, with his height just over six feet, Rosemont would have been considered a giant.

Whereas the Macedonian king in his world had commanded the best army of his day, Rosemont commanded only a company of the foremost military force in his. Even though Echo Company was designated as light infántry, however, it could stand up to a standard infantry battalion in almost anyone's army and grind them into the dust. The Peacekeeper heavy infantry companies could take on a full-strength infantry regiment and wipe them off the face of the earth. The USEF was small, but it was powerful. Man for man, or woman for woman for that matter, they were the best troops in the world. Not even their sister unit, the Russian Expeditionary Force, could stand up to them.

Rosemont had wanted to join the USEF almost from the moment he had been commissioned in the United States Regular Army Infantry, but a slot in the elite unit was hard to get. Of every one hundred men, enlisted or commissioned, who applied to join the Peacekeepers, only three were chosen to don the proud green beret. He had submitted several applications during his service in the Regular Army, but hadn't been selected.

Then came the brief war with the drug lords south of the Mexican border late the previous year. His actions in that campaign had earned him a citation for bravery, but better than that, he had also received an invitation to become a Peacekeeper. He had jumped at the chance and, after breezing through the selection process, had taken over Echo Company just as the USEF deployed to the Middle East for the Mahdi Uprising a little over two months previously.

Though Rosemont had been new to both the USEF and to Echo Company, he had immediately taken to the way the Peacekeepers did business. Unlike the Regular Army, the USEF didn't waste precious time, or even more precious manpower, when it went to war. The Peacekeepers dropped in, quickly assessed the situation and proceeded to kick ass until the situation was back under control. It had been a refreshing way to make war, and he felt comfortable now wearing the green beret. But now that he had been a Peacekeeper for almost three months, he had come to realize that some things were the same in any man's army. And one of those things was a seemingly endless sea of bullshit paperwork that had to be waded through every day.

The way the USEF was organized, the line companies didn't have large headquarters staffs as the Regular Army did. He had an executive officer just as any other infantry company, but when they were in garrison, the XO spent most of his time overseeing the unit's training and maintenance activities rather than handling administrative details. In the field the first sergeant and his small HQ crew took care of the administrative and logistical chores for the unit. But when they were in garrison, there was more than enough left over for the company commander to have to attend to himself.

Rosemont pushed the button on the intercom to the outer office.

"Yes, sir," the voice of his company first sergeant answered instantly.

"Can you come in here a minute, Top?"

"On the way, sir."

The big, burly man with the shaved head who appeared at Rosemont's door an instant later could have been nothing but a professional soldier. First Sergeant Roger "Big Daddy" Ward had been in the Army since he had graduated from high school, and his forty-four-year-old face bore the scars and wrinkles of his twenty-six-year career as an infantryman. The puckered scar that ran along the right side of his jaw had been given to him by a Pakistani bayonet. The matching scar on the left side of his face was courtesy of a piece of grenade frag he'd run into in Colombia. The deep wrinkles around his eyes were from squinting into the sun of more than a dozen battlefields ranging from Egypt to the Amazonian jungle.

His camouflage uniform hid even more physical damage that had been inflicted on him over the years. Anybody who took up the profession of arms had to figure that sometimes those arms would be used against him, as well. But as far as Ward was concerned, what didn't kill him made him a better infantryman.

"Yes, sir."

Rosemont held out a hard copy. "Top, what's this shit about everyone having to go through requalification on unguided heavy weapons?"

The first sergeant shrugged. "The Three Shop thinks that we didn't score enough hits with 'em on our last exercise. They went to the Old Man with it, and he ordered this."

Rosemont shook his head. "Put Lieutenant Sullivan on this ASAP. It's got a short suspense date."

"Is that before or after he finishes the replacement training cycle, sir?"

Rosemont thought for a moment. After the Middle East operation, Echo Company was still short a dozen replacements and he needed those men and women as soon as possible. That meant Sullivan was off the hook this time. "Okay, Top," he sighed. "I'll take care of it myself."

"Yes, sir."

When the first sergeant left, Rosemont went back to the pile of paper on his desk. He was wading through a thick memo on maintenance updates when the Klaxon horn at the end of the hallway went off. Ward instantly reappeared at Rosemont's open door. "Dep Two, sir," he snapped. "Immediate deployment."

Rosemont glanced down at the comlink on his wrist, but the readout was blank. "Where are we going?" he asked.

"Fucked if I know, sir." The scar on Ward's jaw stretched in a grin. "But if I was you, I'd get my little shit together and get the fuck outta my orderly room so I can go to work. Sir!"

Rosemont didn't take offense at Ward's abrasive manner. Like every infantry company commander since the dawn of time, he knew that his first sergeant really ran the company, and when Top said to get moving, it behooved him to evaporate. The last thing Big Daddy needed right now was to have an officer standing around asking stupid questions while he was trying to get Echo Company on its way to war.

"That's most affirm, Top."

WHEN ROSEMONT REACHED his deployment station at Benning's Lawson Airfield, he found that he was almost the last one of his company to arrive. His XO, First Lieutenant Thomas "Mick" Sullivan, was already there with the First Platoon he commanded when they deployed. First Lieutenant Jubal Early Butler "Jeb" Stuart's Second Platoon was all accounted for, as was First Lieutenant Ashley Wells's recon platoon grunts. The only troops not present and accounted for was one of the rocket mortar crews from First Lieutenant Hank Rivera's weapons platoon.

"What's the drill, sir?" Sullivan asked as he walked up to his company commander. "Is this an exercise?" As Echo Company's XO, he was also the unit's unofficial rumor-control officer. Today, however, he had no rumors to work with, since no one seemed to know what was going on.

"Damned if I know, Mick," Rosemont said. "All I know is we're at Dep Two."

Just then the comlink on his wrist beeped that it was receiving a message. He punched in his ID code and quickly scanned the readout. "This is no exercise," he told the officers clustered around him. "We're going to war."

"Where?" Ashley Wells asked in a low but very feminine voice. Even in chameleon camouflage and full battle gear, the slender, blond Ashley Wells was stunningly beautiful. Her beauty, however, didn't mean that she was not a tough, battle-hardened, professional soldier. She was universally known in the Peacekeepers as "Ash-and-Trash." The nickname came not only for her effective use of the more pungent words of the English language, but also for what she left behind at the end of an operation. When Ashley Wells's recon grunts were done with an area, all that was left was ash and trash.

Rosemont looked over at his recon platoon leader. "There's been a coup in the Bantu People's Democracy," he said. "The president's been assassinated and the government's been overthrown."

"What the hell does that have to do with us?" Ashley raised her eyebrows. "I thought we didn't do piss-ant internal disputes."

"Apparently we're making an exception this time," he replied. "A junta led by the vice president, Madame Jewel Jumal, has taken over the country, and she's blaming the white population for the assassination. She's ordered that all the whites are to be rounded up and shot. There's several hundred of them corralled in a sports stadium in Johannesburg, and we're going in to get them out."

Though Rosemont and his officers had been children when what had been the Republic of South Africa became the Bantu People's Democracy some twenty years before, they had all heard the stories of the fate of the minority white population. While the transition from white to black rule hadn't been the bloodbath many had feared, it hadn't been entirely peaceful, either. Since then, though, the several thousand whites who had remained behind after the Boer exodus had lived in harmony with the black population. This incident threatened not only the lives of these people, but also the entire political structure of the nation.

Ashley shook her head in disgust. "Just what I fucking need, a baby-sitting job."

Rosemont laughed. "If it makes you feel any better, I guess I should tell you that the hostages are being guarded by Simbas, the Bantu political troops."

That brought a faint smile to Ashley's lips. "Good. We haven't kicked their asses yet."

Over the South Atlantic, August 12

Alex Rosemont squirmed inside his drop capsule. The C-36B Valkyrie supersonic airborne assault transport had been in the air for more than four hours now, and he was still trying to find a way to get comfortable. As he always did when he waited to make a drop, he was sweating like a pig and would have gladly given a full month's pay and allowances for a hot shower and a cold drink. Although he was fully jump qualified and had made dozens of drops, Rosemont had an almost paralyzing fear of heights and hated airborne drops more than anything else in the world.

He had been able to successfully hide this particular fear throughout his Army career and he was sure as hell not going to let it get the better of him this time, either. Any man who wore a jump badge was allowed to refuse to make a drop whenever he wanted. But doing that would cost him not only his jump wings, but his command of Echo Company, as well. He would make this drop even if it killed him, which was exactly what he was afraid of.

Looking down the row of half-opened drop capsules on the opposite side of the plane, he saw that unlike himself, most of the recon grunts were sound asleep. He had never been able to nap on the way to the drop zone and resented their veteran nonchalance. At the head of her Strider Alpha recon team, he spotted the glitter of the silver skull earring in Sergeant Kat Wallenska's right ear and smiled to himself.

At the conclusion of the Middle East operation, Rosemont had taken a week's R and R in Spain. It had just so happened that Kat Wallenska had chosen to take her R and R at the same place. Actually it had been Kat's stated choice rather than mere chance that had brought them together for that week. Both of them knew the risks that went along with an officer and an NCO becoming romantically involved in a military environment and neither one of them wanted that. They were both too dedicated to their profession to even have time for an affair. But R and R was time out, and they had used the time well.

When the week was up, they had parted to return to their jobs. Since then his relationship with the recon sergeant had been purely business, as he had known it would be, but he savored the memory of that week anyway. Maybe someday in the future, they would have a chance to take R and R together again. The thought took his mind off his present situation for a moment. But not for long, though.

AT THE FRONT of the row of seats opposite Rosemont, Ashley Wells watched her company commander as his eyes scanned the line of grunts. The recon platoon leader saw his eyes stop and linger on Kat Wallenska for a moment before moving on. A flash of anger shot through her, but she forced it down.

Like everyone else in Echo Company, Ashley knew that Rosemont had spent his R and R with Kat Walenska. There was nothing in the Peacekeeper regulations that prohibited sexual relations between the men and women in the unit as long as they didn't affect their duty performance. She didn't have any designs on Rosemont, or on Kat for that matter, but she still resented their closeness. She saw it as detracting Rosemont's attention from her and she hated anything that took attention away from herself.

Ashley Wells was ambitious, but she hadn't joined the Peacekeepers to have a job. She'd had all the civilian job she could possibly handle just trying to spend her share of her family's money. She had taken a commission in the Regular Army and later joined the Peacekeepers because she wanted to be known for doing something more useful than spending money. The problem was that since she was one of the many daughters of Winston W. Wells III, the UniCard banking tycoon, people had not taken her choice of a military career seriously. No one understood why a woman like her would want to give up a life of wealth and comfort for the Spartan existence of a professional soldier.

Because of that, becoming a Peacekeeper had been very difficult for her, but she had pursued it with the same dogged determination that had made her father one of the wealthiest men in the world. And she had been successful, very successful. She had earned her nickname a dozen times over on twice as many battlefields. She had an outstanding record in the Peacekeepers and was on the fast track to an early promotion to captain. The last thing she needed was to have her company commander involved with one of her sergeants.

The problem was that she hadn't gotten off on the right foot with Rosemont when he took command of Echo Company at the beginning of the Middle Eastern operation. If fact, they had clashed so badly that he had finally threatened to have her transferred out of the unit if she didn't back down and cooperate with him.

Ashley wasn't the most introspective woman in the world and she was totally unaware of what had caused the clash. To the other officers in Echo Company, however, it was obvious. The ambitious, aristocratic blonde was a superstar in the USEF and she expected to be treated that way, as much for her stunning beauty as for her outstanding military prowess. Being new to the USEF, and to his recon platoon leader's sterling reputation both as a woman and a soldier, Rosemont had treated her the same as all his personnel, and that hadn't sat well with Ashley Wells.

How much of her clash with him had come about because he hadn't succumbed to her beauty and how much because he hadn't bowed to what she saw as her superior military experience, she wasn't aware of. All she knew was that he had threatened to fire her as if she were some malfunctioning recruit. For the first time in her military career, her good looks hadn't been enough to sway someone. She'd had to back down and toe the line. She was determined that she wasn't going to give Rosemont any excuse to get rid of her in the future. There was no way in hell that she was going to let that man get the better of her.

SINCE HE COULDN'T SLEEP, Rosemont replayed the operation plan on his tac display one more time and checked to see if any updates had been posted on his comlink. The plan was simple and straightforward. Rosemont and the recon platoon would hit the DZ at daybreak and clear it before the rest of the company came in. Then, once Echo Company had the area around the DZ firmly under control, the aviation company would land and the rescue operation would begin. If everything went as planned, they would free the white hostages, evacuate them to the airfield and be on their way back to Benning by nightfall.

He was fully aware, though, that the first cardinal rule of warfare was that no operational plan ever survived the initial contact with the enemy. The Bantu People's Democracy had the largest, best-equipped army in southern Africa. Much of the revenues from the nation's extensive gold and diamond mines and mineral resources for the past several years had gone into military hardware, and the results were impressive.

Force Intel had reported that most of the Bantu National Army and the Simba political troops were deployed along the borders with their warring neighbors. But he knew that situation could change quickly. The Simbas were highly mobile and, once they learned of the Peacekeeper operation, could shift forces to oppose them rapidly. He would have been a little more comfortable if the rest of the USEF was going to be close by in case something went tits up. But due to a threatening situation in Brazil that required holding some of the Peacekeepers in reserve, the colonel had felt the hostage situation didn't merit deploying the entire USEF.

Since Rosemont wouldn't know what the real situation was until they hit the DZ, all he could do was try to relax like the rest of his troops.

ROSEMONT HEARD the electric whine of the Valkyrie's wing-sweep motors and felt the drop ship suddenly decelerate as it went subsonic. The only good thing he had to say about the supersonic, swing-wing transport plane was that it got him to the drop zone quickly and didn't drag out the agony.

Flicking on his nav display, he saw that they had just crossed the coast and were heading inland. The drop zone, a small airfield cleared out of the bush on the outskirts of Jo'burg, would be coming up soon and once more he would jump out of a perfectly good airplane. He felt the sweat break out again and would have killed for a shower.

When the "suit up" signal sounded in his earphones, he closed the jump capsule shell around his chest and dogged it down tight. Dropping his helmet visor, he checked the helmet seals and turned on the oxygen supply he would use on the drop. The dry, stale taste of the bottled air made him salivate, and he swallowed to clear his mouth.

God, he hated this shit!

After making a last function check on the drop capsule, he stood at the end of the jump line and shuffled forward to the capsule launchers on the sides of the aircraft. The display on his visor still read that everything was in the green as he stepped back into the launcher. He felt the clamps secure him and the magnoelastic joints of his capsule stiffen to lock his legs together and hold his arms tightly to his sides.

He was on the end of the stick and had to wait until the rest of the recon platoon was launched before he felt the slam of the launch against his shoulders. As always, his stomach lurched and he clamped his jaws together, sucking in the stale, dry oxygen as deeply as he could as the capsule bounced in the plane's turbulence when it cleared the launcher.

When the stabilizers snapped out and caught the air to smooth his descent, Rosemont called up the drop display on his visor and watched the altimeter reading swiftly count down. Although he had made two drops with the recon platoon on his first Peacekeeper operation, he was still not used to the kamikaze-style descent they always used when they dropped. His speed was within the safety limits for a recon capsule, but dangerously on the high side.

He rested his right index finger on the trigger for the speed brakes, but didn't pop a retard. Right now his capsule was as stealthy as was technologically possible to make it. His radar signature was less than a small-sized sparrow's, but the instant that he hit the retards, he would show up as if he were in a metal hot-air balloon. Force Intel had claimed that the airfield didn't have a radar powerful enough to pick them up on the way down, but he wasn't taking any chances. Intel had been proven to be wrong before.

As the altimeter numbers counted down almost too fast for the eye to follow, he watched the other capsules on his screen. They were approaching the deploy point at almost three hundred miles per hour, but no one had popped his canopy yet. He felt his testicles suck up into his groin when he thought of hitting the ground at that speed.

When he saw the lead capsule pop its main chute, he instinctively triggered his own. The opening shock slammed him against the capsule shell, but it was over in an instant as the breaking chute fully deployed.

The instant his chute came open, the threat warning shrieked in his ear. Antiaircraft gun radar was painting the recon capsules!

A stream of red tracer fire reached up from the ground and brushed past the capsules below him. In the thin light of dawn, he saw the antlike figures of men raising their weapons as more tracer fire streaked up at them.

Demagging his capsule joints to free his arms, he unclipped his M-25 Light Assault Rifle from its mount on the right side of his capsule. A recon grunt's 5 mm LAR wasn't the best weapon in the world for this situation, but since it was all he had, it just had to do.

His thumb flicked the selector switch down to full auto as his finger tightened on the trigger. He had a hundred rounds of 5 mm caseless ammunition in the cylindrical plastic magazine clipped in place at the end of the weapon's breech, but at the full-auto rate of fire—800 rounds a minute—it wouldn't last very long.

Using the optical sights, he zeroed in on a group of men running for a sandbagged gun pit hidden in the scrub brush at the end of the airstrip and triggered off a long burst. His aim was true, and three of them went down. The others abruptly turned around and tried to run back for cover inside the two hangars at the edge of the runway, but fire from another capsule cut them down in midstride.

For the next few seconds, it was a free-for-all in the sky over the drop zone as more ground fire opened up. The recon capsules weren't armored like the heavy infantry Hulk suits, but they could still withstand most small-arms fire. And since the grunts were wearing their full armor inserts in the field uniforms, the rounds that did pierce the capsules did little serious damage to their occupants.

Several of the grunts sustained damage to their canopies and made hard landings, but once the capsules were on the ground, it was an entirely different story. On the ground the recon grunts were in their element. Quickly forming up into their teams, they went into fire and maneuver, their LARs blazing. The hostiles at the airstrip were stunned by the assault, but tried to counterattack.

Rosemont found himself alone when he shrugged out of his capsule. In the dim light of dawn, indistinct figures raced toward him, their weapons firing. He rolled behind his empty capsule and, when the IFF on his tac display didn't mark them as friendlies, zeroed in on them. Now that he could use his LAR's laser sight, he switched the rifle over to the 3-round-burst mode.

His first burst took the lead hostile in the chest. The high-velocity 5 mm rounds ripped through him and dropped him dead in his tracks. Several rounds of return fire sang past Rosemont's head and more hit his empty capsule. Triggering off two more short bursts, he sent two more men to the ground, and the remaining hostiles broke off and raced for cover. Getting to his feet, he sent a long burst after them and was rewarded by seeing one more of them go down.

Checking his tac display, Rosemont saw the locator beacons of Strider Charlie over to his left. Flashing his intentions to the team leader, he quickly joined up with them as they got busy clearing out the scattered pockets of hostiles. Now that they had gained fire superiority, the mopping up went quickly. None of the hostiles surrendered, but those who didn't die fled into the brush, and the ceasefire command was soon flashed to the grunts.

Silence finally fell over the airfield, broken only by the crackling flames from the burning hangars. Gunfire had ignited something in the buildings, and the flames had quickly spread. Several Peacekeepers were fighting the flames, not really because they wanted to save the buildings, but to keep the column of smoke from announcing their presence.

Not that their airborne landing could be kept a secret. A quick count showed two dozen hostile bodies in the area, but several more had escaped into the scrub brush around the airstrip. So much for secrecy and Force Intel's information about what they were facing.

It had not been a good way to start the day.

Malaika airfield, August 12

A dirty, smoke-stained Lieutenant Ashley Wells walked up to Alex Rosemont. The muzzle of the LAR in her hand trailed a thin tendril of smoke in the cool morning air. Following close behind her was Sergeant Kat Wallenska.

"Major," Wells said, pointing to the still-smoldering hangars at the edge of the airstrip. "Sergeant Wallenska found something over there I think you ought to take a look at."

Sergeant John Ironstone, Wallenska's assistant team leader, was waiting for him at the hangar, his open visor showing his dark, copper-colored skin and blue-black hair. A Comanche from outside Oklahoma City, Ironstone considered himself to be a modern Indian warrior following a long, proud Comanche tradition. He didn't ride a horse to war, but the skimmers, Tilt Wings and drop capsules that carried him to battle were far faster than any horse, and his LAR reached farther than the most powerful bow.

He did, however, follow the Comanche tradition of wearing war paint on his face when he went on operations. Three broad, upward-slanting black stripes adorned each of his cheeks. No one could see the stripes when his helmet visor was down, but he knew they were there and that was what really mattered. The war paint was his honor and strength, and he would have no more considered going into battle without it than he would leaving his assault rifle behind.

"They left us a present, sir," he said with a grin, pointing to a hulking shape resting on the concrete at the other end of the hangar.

Even though it was burned, as well, Rosemont could make out the deadly form of a Mangusta V helicopter gunship. The nose of the ship was untouched by the fire and painted on the green, purple and black camouflage, he saw the crossed panga knives and death's-head insignia of the People's Democratic Movement political troops, the Simbas. He had been given an extensive background briefing on the Simbas on the flight across the Atlantic and knew they were a threat not to be taken lightly.

"Force Intel didn't tell us anything about having to face this shit," Wells said. "According to those malfs, all the Simba air assets are stationed along their borders with Namibia, Mozambique and Zimbabwe. This was supposed to be a purely civilian airfield." She shook her head. "First the troops and the antiaircraft guns, and now this."

"And if you'll look over here, sir," Wallenska broke in on Ashley's muttering, "you can see that they're set up to service another gunship in this hangar, as well as two more over in the other building."

Having hostile gunships in his area of operations would make a big difference in the conduct of the mission. Since the entire Expeditionary Force wasn't being deployed this time, he had only limited air assets and most of them were the transport aircraft that were needed to evacuate the hostages. He did have a section of four armed Bubble Top scout ships coming in, but they wouldn't be much help if the hostiles decided to hit them with a fleet of Mangusta gunships.

"I'd better get on the horn back to Benning about this," Rosemont said. "If we're up against gunships, we're going to need some more help."

"It'd be real helpful if they could send us some Broad Arrows, sir," Kat said, referring to the potent British antiaircraft missiles they had encountered in hostile hands during their recent operation in the Middle East. Using an advanced low-IR-seeking guidance system coupled to a vectored-thrust rocket motor, they were the perfect weapon for taking on chopper gunships.

"I don't think they can help us with them," Rosemont said. The British were still denying all knowledge of the advanced missiles even though some had been captured in Iran. "But hopefully we can get a few more Wasps in to supplement what we have on hand."

Echo Company's basic combat load included a dozen Wasp shoulder-fired antiaircraft missiles, but they wouldn't be enough to deal with a major Simba air attack. Also the Wasp wasn't the best antiaircraft missile in the world. In an organization that prided itself on having the best weapons modern technology could produce, the one glaring exception in the Peacekeeper arsenal was the Wasp. The failure of the proposed Yellow Jacket missile, which had been ordered as a replacement for the Wasps, left them with a second-rate air-defense system.

"Until then, however," he told Ashley, "keep your people on their toes and get an air watch with our Wasps set up on the perimeter. Then let's finish securing this place so we can get the rest of the troops down."

"Yes, sir."

LIEUTENANT MICK SULLIVAN stepped out of his drop capsule and looked around the airfield. So far, except for the unexpected reception committee, the drop had gone like an exercise back at Benning. Sullivan's First Platoon grunts were all down and were moving into their perimeter defensive positions. Stuart's Second Platoon grunts were still under their canopies, and the weapons platoon capsules were just leaving the launchers in their Valkyrie. In another few minutes, the entire company would be on the ground and ready to go to work.

Sullivan found his company commander over by the burned-out hangars with Ashley Wells and Kat Wallenska. "Yo, Major!" he greeted Rosemont. "This is looking more and more like that scene out of *Wild Geese,* with Richard Burton and Roger Moore. You know, the scene where they take that airfield after freeing the African president from prison."

Rosemont smiled. Sullivan was well-known as a fanatic follower of old flatvee movies. His specialty was old war movies and, at the drop of a hat, he could deliver an hour's lecture on any topic from the John Wayne Cavalry-Indian war movies to Rambo as a symbol of urban social unrest in late-twentieth-century American society. Obviously he'd been brushing up on his classic African mercenary movies recently.

"I saw that one, too," Rosemont replied. "If I remember it correctly, they captured the airfield okay. But the plane didn't come in to pick them up, and they had to make a run for it."

"That's right, sir," Sullivan said. "They missed the plane and had to walk out. But this sure looks like the same place they filmed."

"The planes had sure as hell better show up for us," Ashley growled, her eyes flicking over to the burned-out hulk of the Simba helicopter in the hangar. "Intel has already fucked up enough on this mission. We don't need any more little surprises."

"That's a fact," Rosemont agreed. "So let's get the Bats in the air so we can see what we're dealing with here."

Included in the supplies that had been dropped to support the operation were two ground-launch versions of the UAV-15C Bat Unmanned Aerial Vehicle. Powered by a fully shielded, high-thrust miniature turbine, the three-meter-wide recon flyers carried a full battery of sensors, detectors and jammers in their bellies. With the "mirror skin" covering that could change color to match the sky it flew through, the IR shielding on its jet exhaust and its radar jammers, the Bat was almost impossible to detect with anything but the most sophisticated sensors.

The Bat ground-support crew swarmed over the two flyers, fueling them and checking the data links from the sensors and detectors. As soon as the first flyer was ready, it was hoisted up into the cradle of its zero-length launcher and the jet engine started. Once the exhaust-gas temperature was in the green, the UAV controller spooled the small turbine up to full power and punched the button that fired the rocket-assist takeoff unit.

The Bat leaped from its launcher with a roar and quickly climbed to altitude. The controller held the flyer in a tight orbit over the airfield as he ran through a last series of systems checks. When they were completed, he sent the recon bird speeding for Jo'burg.

HALF AN HOUR LATER, Rosemont and his officers clustered around the UAV monitor in the jump CP that had been set up in one of the burned-out hangars. The monitor was linked to the Bat flying over Johannesburg, and the images being relayed from the small recon flyer were as good a depiction of the area it was flying over as they would have gotten from a low-level Bubble Top recon flight. Actually it was better. The flyer's multispectrum sensors and detectors could see what the naked eye could not. Specifically they could see through even the most artful camouflage and detect whatever was hiding underneath it.

Right now the Bat was circling at two thousand feet over the southeastern suburbs of the city looking down at the People's Sports Stadium, which had been pressed into service as a concentration camp for the white hostages. The small recon vehicle's skin was dialed to light blue, rendering it invisible against the morning sky. The electronic countermeasures jammers in its belly also made it invisible to all spectra of radar detection including the radars directing the battery of antiaircraft missiles ringing the stadium. Though the missile radars couldn't see the flyer, to the Bat's sensors, the camouflaged missile launchers couldn't have been any plainer if they'd had laser hologram signs erected over them.

"We're sure as hell not going to just fly in there and get those people out with those missiles down there," Sullivan said, stating the obvious.

Rosemont could only agree. The mission plan called for a lightning air assault to secure a beachhead at the stadium. Once it was in the Peacekeepers' hands, the captives would be flown to the safety of the airfield and further evacuated from there. With the missiles around the stadium, however, the mission plan would have to be scrapped. Even if he'd had twice as many gunships at his command as he did, there was no way that he could follow the plan without taking unacceptable casualties. The Peacekeepers would die when it was necessary for them to die, but he wasn't about to throw their lives away.

"This is rapidly turning into a world-class dog fuck," he growled. "We're back to square one."

Ashley Wells smiled to herself. The new company commander was sounding more and more like her every day. Maybe there was some hope for him after all.

"Okay, people," Rosemont said with a last glance at the Bat's readouts. "We've got to get this operation back on track quickly. Obviously the planned air assault is out. We're going to have to go in there on foot and knock out the missiles before we can fly in and get those people out."

He turned to First Lieutenant Jubal "Jeb" Stuart, his Second Platoon leader. "Jeb, get your people ready to move out ASAP. I'll lift you halfway there in our two Tilt Wings, but you'll have to go the rest of the way on foot."

Stuart nodded. "Yes, sir."

"Mick," Rosemont continued, "your people will stay here and secure this place."

The XO nodded. He had expected that, on a mission like this, the other guys would always have all the fun.

"Ashley, I want you to detach two of your teams to go with Jeb."

"Yes, sir."

MADAME JEWEL JUMAL, the acting president of the Bantu People's Democracy, studied the large-scale topographic map of Johannesburg mounted on the wall of the operations room. Following the assassination of President Bolothu four days before, she had moved her office into the command center of her party's headquarters building in the nation's capital of Pretoria so she could better control the consolidation of power in the hands of her People's Democratic Movement.

Madame Jumal was aristocratically tall and slim. Her light skin and golden eyes told of North African Arabic blood somewhere in her ancestry. Her long, dark brown hair fell free in a wavy cascade over her shoulders. Had she been dressed in fashionable European clothing, she could have passed without undue notice in any metropolitan European capital. But in her colorful African attire, she would be taken for nothing except what she was, a powerful African woman and the leader of the People's Democratic

Movement, which was now in firm control of the Bantu People's Democracy.

Madame Jumal hadn't reached her position of power by being weak, nor had she done it by being afraid of spilling blood. Her rise to the leadership of the People's Democratic Movement had been marked by a long trail of blood, but the coalition government she had been forced into with the late President Bolothu had temporarily ended the bloodshed. Bolothu had always hated to kill and, as far as Jumal was concerned, that had been his greatest weakness.

Bolothu's assassination had ended the uneasy truce between the two major black parties and the white minority. The nation's constitution made her the acting president, but when she was finished eliminating the opposition parties, she would be the sole leader of the nation. The assassination had also given her a welcome opportunity to rid the country of the last of the hated whites, and she would allow nothing to stop her plans. Certainly not the American Peacekeepers.

Their landing at the Malaika airfield had been a surprise, but it wouldn't be a setback to her plans. The reports indicated that there was only a small force of them, not enough to be taken seriously—not when she commanded the largest and best-equipped military force in all of southern Africa, her Simbas.

Standing a respectful distance away at the end of the command center was a group of men wearing green, purple and black tiger-stripe camouflage field uniforms. Maroon berets bearing silver crossed panga knives and death's-head badges were folded under their left epaulets. The badges were those of the feared Simba Impis, the armed regiments of her People's

Democratic Movement. The Simbas had originally been formed as an armed bodyguard for the leaders of the party, but now they were the foremost military force in the nation. Outnumbering the Bantu National Army by almost two to one, the Simbas were not only armed with the most modern weapons that money could buy, but they were also well trained in their use and were fanatically loyal to their female leader.

She looked over and locked eyes with one of the Simba officers, a battalion commander, and he stiffened to a rigid position of attention. "I want you," she said, "to stop the Americans before they leave the airstrip. Do not allow them into Johannesburg."

The Simba saluted her with a raised clenched fist and quickly departed.

Jumal's piercing golden eyes swept over the other men. The Simbas met her gaze squarely and unflinchingly. Not to do so was taken as a sign of weakness and Madame Jumal didn't tolerate weakness in her Simbas.

"The rest of you are to ready your men and move them into the city. It is time that we rid our lands of the white contamination."

The Simba officers saluted and marched out of her office.

5

In the Bush, August 12

Kat Wallenska peered around the edge of the thornbush, her LAR ready in her hands. The shack at the edge of the dirt road had been a small tavern, judging by the cases of empty beer bottles littering the ground behind the building. If it had once been a beer joint, it looked deserted now like everything else they had seen so far on their way into Jo'burg. Even in the Tilt Wings during their flight into the landing zone twenty kilometers outside the city limits, they had seen no signs of life in the scattered farms and villages they had flown over.

Whatever was going on in the city had sent everyone in the surrounding area running for deep cover. The only people they had seen so far had been in the distance and they had been heading away from the city as fast as they could go. That was good, but now that they were approaching the outskirts of the inhabited area they would have to be even more cautious.

"Alpha One One," she spoke into her implant. "One Zero. I've got a shack at the side of the road at one o'clock. Move in and check it out."

“One One,” came Ironstone’s voice over her earphones. “Affirm.”

Two figures detached themselves from the brush to her left and darted toward the shack. As they ran, their chameleon camouflage suits shifted colors, blending them in with the parched summer colors of the African bush. One of the grunts stopped and pressed himself against the wall by the open front of the building while the other one slipped inside.

“One Zero, One One,” Ironstone reported a moment later. “It’s clear.”

“Affirm, we’re coming up.”

Wallenska got to her feet and signaled for the rest of the team to move up. Even though it slowed their march to stop and check every hut and shack in their way, she couldn’t let anything pass without clearing it.

HALF A KILOMETER behind Kat’s fast-moving recon team, Lieutenant Jeb Stuart’s Second Platoon ran at a dogtrot. Once known as the “Airborne Shuffle”, the grunts could keep up this ground-eating pace all day long, slowing to a walk only ten minutes out of every hour to rest. Moving at this pace, they could cover eight kilometers every hour and not be exhausted if they had to stop and fight.

Most of his friends thought that Stuart had been named after the famous General Jeb Stuart, even though his first three names were different from the Confederate cavalry officer with the same initials and last name. Being a son of the Old South, however, he didn’t mind that assumption at all. In fact, his first two names, Jubal Early, were those of another, less distinguished Confederate general his family claimed descent from. His third name, Butler, however, was from his mother's side of the family and had nothing to do with the American Civil War, or "The War Between the States," as real Southerners still preferred to call it.

The situation unfolding on Stuart's tac display on the inside of his helmet visor was right out of the exploits of General Jeb Stuart—a cavalry raid deep into enemy-held territory. The difference was that this time, he and his Second Platoon were racing for their objective on foot, not mounted on horseback. That was a good thing, however, as this Jeb Stuart had never been on a horse in his entire life.

So far, the mission had been a walk in the sun, but Stuart wasn't about to relax yet. He knew how quickly a situation like this could turn to pure dog shit. Since Force Intel had been dead wrong about the conditions at the airfield drop zone, they could be equally wrong about the situation around Jo'burg.

He would have felt much more comfortable if they had made some kind of contact with the Simbas. Nothing too big to slow them down, of course, but he always felt better if he knew exactly where the opposition was and what they were doing. This way, having to depend entirely on the recon teams to scout the route for him, he was left hanging until they found the hostiles for him.

The sun-baked scrub brush they were moving through looked deceptively sparse, but it was actually quite thick in places. Thick enough to hide a fairly large force. Now that the African sun was high overhead, shimmering heat mirages further cut his visibility to a mere few hundred meters in most directions.

With the ambient air temperature close to body temperature, the IR sensors gave suspect readings. For all the sophisticated equipment his troops carried, Stuart realized that in this setting he might as well be back in the spear-and-shield era of warfare. It was not a comforting thought.

JEB STUART HAD his wish, and now he knew where the hostiles were. As often happens with wishes, now he wished that he had kept his fat mouth shut. Dozens of Simbas had suddenly appeared from the brush on his left flank, their weapons blazing. How Kat's recon team had missed them he didn't know, but it didn't really matter now. The shit was in the fan, and he had to deal with it.

The grunts reacted quickly, diving for cover and setting up a base of counterambush fire. But the Simbas brushed it off and pressed their assault behind a hail of automatic-weapons fire. And it sure as hell wasn't second-rate Han Empire stuff they were throwing at them, either. From the sound of the hostile small-arms fire, the Simbas were equipped with Singapore copies of the American-designed 5 mm LARs. If the bastards were equipped with copies of the laser sights, as well, they were going to be in deep shit.

Stuart was on the comlink back to Rosemont at the airfield CP instantly. "Bold Lancer, Bold Cowboy," he transmitted. "We have contact."

"Lancer, flash it."

Stuart keyed his data pad, sending his sensor and imager readouts of the attacking force back to Rosemont. When the company commander acknowledged the data, he continued his report. "They're Simbas," he said. "There's no doubt about that, and they're coming on strong and we're taking casualties. From what I can see, we're facing at least three companies."

"Can you pull back?"

"Only if we can get some fire support," the platoon leader replied. "They're pressing us hard."

"Affirm, go directly to Bold Thunder."

"Bold Thunder, Bold Cowboy," Stuart transmitted to Hank Rivera's weapons platoon FDC. "Fire mission. Troops in the open, will control."

"Cowboy, Thunder," the Fire Direction Center answered. "Flash it."

Stuart flashed his target coordinates to the FDC fire-support computers. The FDC instantly relayed the locations to the rocket mortar battery, and the first round was out of the tube in under ten seconds. Three more followed almost instantly.

"Cowboy, Thunder," the FDC called. "Rounds on the way. Transferring control to you now."

"Cowboy, affirm." Stuart locked his imager on the center mass of the assaulting Simba infantry and punched in the fire-support code on his keypad. Halfway through its trajectory, the first rocket mortar round streaking through the sky linked with Stuart's imager and corrected its flight path to impact exactly where the platoon leader wanted it to hit. The rocket projectile also switched its multipurpose warhead over to antipersonnel effect when Stuart keyed in the warhead function code.

The first round detonated a hundred meters above the scrub brush. The enhanced high-explosive warhead sent hundreds of red-hot shards of razor-sharp steel raining down on the Simbas. Caught out in the open with no effective overhead cover, they were swatted down like flies. The next two rounds followed seconds later and added to the carnage.

Under the protective hail of killing steel, Stuart started withdrawing his troops, taking his wounded with him. But the Simbas didn't back off and let them get away clean. For every man who was cut down by the air bursts, two more took his place.

KAT LAY in the dust of a small, brushy knoll on Stuart's right flank, covering the withdrawal of her team with carefully aimed shots. From the hurried hypno implant she had received on the flight over the Atlantic, she knew that the small hill would be called a *kopje* in Afrikaans, the language of the white Boers. Why she hadn't been fed a hypno on Bantu, the major black language in the region, she had no idea. Obviously Force Intel had felt that they wouldn't be making significant contact with the black population during the rescue mission.

But once again, Intel had severely stepped on their foreskins with golf shoes.

The troops in the black, purple and green tiger-stripe camouflage uniforms swarming all over Second Platoon sure as hell weren't white Boers. They were Simbas, the fanatic black troops of Jumal's People's Democratic Movement. Well armed and well trained, they were a force to be reckoned with, as Stuart's grunts were learning.

Kat's team had been reconning Stuart's right flank when the Simbas suddenly appeared out of the scrub brush screaming their battle cries. For the first few minutes the recon grunts went to ground, returned fire and waited for the pattern of the enemy attack to reveal itself. But now it was all too apparent that there was no maneuver plan to the attack. It was simply a headlong assault using the Simba's superior numbers to try to overwhelm the Second Platoon. Now that Stuart was withdrawing under the cover of the mortar barrage, she had to pull her people back too, before they were cut off.

When the bolt on Kat's LAR locked back on an empty magazine, she reached down to her ammo pouch for a fresh one and caught a flash of movement out of the corner of her eye. With a bloodcurdling cry, a Simba launched himself out of the brush a few meters to her left, his deadly panga knife raised overhead to deliver a killing blow.

With no time to reload her rifle, Kat snatched the fighting knife from the sheath on her boot and rolled into her attacker. The panga flashed through the air behind her as she stabbed upward, her knife sinking to the hilt into the Simba's groin. She gave the blade a savage twist, severing his femoral artery.

The Simba gave a scream and tried to raise his panga again, but the sudden loss of blood pressure stopped him in his tracks. He dropped to the ground beside her and was dead in less than sixty seconds.

As she had told the trainees in the edged-weapons class just the day before, the object of the exercise was to kill the fucker, not dance with him.

Wiping the blade clean on the Simba's camouflage jacket, she sheathed the knife and retrieved her LAR. Clipping a fresh 100-round plastic magazine in place, she pulled back on the charging handle to chamber the first round. Now where were the rest of those bastards?

BACK AT HIS AIRFIELD CP, Rosemont studied the tac display on the master monitor. Even with the covering fire of Rivera's rocket mortar battery, Stuart was hard-pressed as he tried to break contact. The mortars were cycling through the ammunition as fast as the gunners could load the feed trays, but it wasn't enough. The Simbas were taking serious casualties, but they kept on coming.

He saw that Stuart was withdrawing his grunts to a decent defensive location, a small rise in the ground with good fields of fire. But holding the high ground wouldn't be enough to save them if the Simbas kept on coming.

"Yo! Hansen!" Rosemont called over to the captain commanding the aviation section. "Jeb's got his ass in a crack. How fast can you get your Bubble Tops in the air?"

The scout ships had arrived right as Jeb had moved out, and the ground crews were swarming over them, fueling and loading ammunition. Hansen glanced down at his comlink to check the status of his aircraft. "They're just finishing arming the last one, Major. We can crank immediately."

"Affirm. Get 'em going."

"We're on the way."

"Bold Cowboy," Rosemont transmitted to the beleaguered Stuart. "Bold Lancer."

"Cowboy, go."

"Lancer. Find a place to hole up, Jeb. I'm sending the gunships in."

"That's most affirm," Stuart said, relief evident in his voice. "Get 'em coming ASAP, Lancer. We can't hold them back much longer."

"They're cranking now."

USEF First Lieutenant "Gunner" Thompson nudged the cyclic control of his Bubble Top forward, dropping the nose of the ship even lower over the brush-covered plain. Twisting the throttle up hard against the stop, he nursed every last mile per hour he could get out of the screaming turbine. The small recon scout ship was only fifty feet above the ground, flying flat out at well over two hundred and fifty miles per hour.

The other three ships of the aerial scout section were flying line astern of their flight leader, following him as if they were tied together with string. Second Platoon was up to their asses in alligators, and Talon Flight was in a hurry to start draining the swamp for them.

"Bold Cowboy," Gunner transmitted. "This is Hook Talon Lead. We are inbound to your location, echo tango alpha zero two."

"Cowboy, affirm," Stuart sent back. "I've got hostiles on three sides of me and they're moving around to my rear. We can sure as hell use a little assistance around here."

Thompson grinned broadly behind his helmet visor. "That's most affirm, Cowboy. It's on the way." Gunner was his name, and high-speed, low-altitude ass-kicking was his game.

The OH-39 NOTAR—no tail rotor—Bubble Top scout ship was not only fast, but it was also the most maneuverable helicopter that had ever been built. The combination of the rigid main rotor and jet-thrust directional control design allowed the chopper to do things that had once been the sole privilege of small fixed-wing aerobatic aircraft.

And along with the scout ship's high speed and high maneuverability went a full package of both recon sensors and ground-attack weapons. They didn't carry the massive firepower of the bigger Tilt Wing gunships, but the Bubble Tops were perfect for this kind of close-in, ground-support fire missions.

Today Thompson was loaded with full pods of Long Lash missiles fitted with antipersonnel warheads under his stub wings and EHE fragmentation rounds loaded in his 20 mm chain gun ammunition bays. He was ready to go to work. All he needed was a target.

6

In the Brush, August 12

Seeing Stuart's hilltop position rapidly approaching, Gunner Thompson chopped his Bubble Top's throttle, dropped down even lower over the scrub brush and deployed his MAADS, the rotor mast acquisition and detection system. Extending a meter above the rotor disk when it was fully deployed, this sensor system allowed him to look over the top of the small hill without exposing the scout ship to enemy observation and fire.

"Bingo!" Thompson called out when he saw the target readouts of his tacscreen. "I've got your customers, Jeb. Keep your heads down, we're coming in."

"That's affirm, Gunner," Stuart sent back. "Get 'em off us."

"Stay frosty, Jeb. We're on 'em."

"Talon Flight, this is Lead," he transmitted as he flashed the target locations to the other three ships. "I don't see any triple-A or missiles, so let's get in there, break 'em up and send 'em home."

A chorus of "affirms" came in as the other three Bubble Tops scattered to attack their targets.

Snapping his ship over into a hard-banked right turn, Talon Lead bore down on his first target, a mass of Simbas assaulting Stuart's left front. A light touch on the chain gun trigger sent fifty rounds of 20 mm EHE into the Simba ranks. Since the Bubble Top was in a skidding turn when he fired, the enhanced high-explosive rounds cut across their front like a scythe. Every exploding round sent dozens of razor-sharp shell fragments slicing into their bodies and stopped the attack dead in its tracks. A heavy volley of fire from the embattled grunts sent the survivors back into the brush.

Thompson's next target was a light machine gun emplaced behind a fallen tree trunk. Locking on to the heat radiating from the gun's muzzle blast, he fired a Long Lash missile from his starboard underwing pod. The instant the missile was free, he banked away sharply to evade the ground fire coming up at him.

The fire-and-forget missile sped on its way, vectoring its thrust nozzle to make a slight course correction as it guided itself into the target. It impacted directly in front of the machine-gun position and detonated with a fiery blast. The explosion shredded both the gun and its crew.

Snapping the tail of his ship around in a hard skidding turn, Thompson started back across Second Platoon's front. Again his chain gun spit 20 mm flame, and the Long Lash missiles reached out with deadly fire-and-forget accuracy. The ground fire was erratic, but he felt his small chopper take several hits. A quick glance at his instrument readouts showed him that all of his systems were still in the green, and he continued pressing his attack.

While Talon Lead worked the front of Stuart's positions, the other three Bubble Tops of Talon Flight were also gainfully employed. One of them worked Stuart's right flank and one worked his left. The third ship stayed high, seeking out targets of opportunity and there were plenty of those. Every time Talon Four spotted a danger, he dived down, chain gun and rocket pods blazing.

Faced with the relentless aerial assault, the stunned Simbas finally broke. Leaving their dead and wounded where they lay, the survivors scattered back into the scrub brush as fast as they could go.

"Cowboy," Thompson called down to Stuart. "Talon Lead. We're going to chase them into the brush for you. I'll leave Talon Four on station in case we missed anyone close in."

"Thanks, Talon, I owe you one."

"Anytime, Cowboy. You can thank me at the club when we get home."

For the first time that morning Stuart chuckled. "That's most affirm, Talon."

WHILE TALON FLIGHT CHASED the Simbas into the brush, back at his airfield CP Rosemont made a quick command decision. The original operations plan had been out the window from the moment they hit the airstrip DZ and discovered their Simba reception committee. Now that Stuart's platoon had made contact, the hostiles were definitely aware that they were operating in their backyard. The original concept of sneaking in and grabbing the hostages out from under their noses would never work now. The only chance he had to pull it off was to go for it with everything he had at his disposal.

That would be risky to both the white hostages and his own people, but he didn't have the time or enough forces at hand to put something else together. And since the longer he waited the less chance he had of pulling it off at all, he had better do it instantly.

He keyed his comlink and called Sullivan. "Bold Racer, Lancer."

"Racer, go."

"Get 'em suited up, Mick," Rosemont said. "We're moving out in zero two."

"Where're we going?"

"We're going to link up with Jeb and drive on into the city."

"Oh, shit!"

"Get 'em moving," Rosemont growled.

MADAME JEWEL JUMAL didn't kill the Simba communications officer who brought her the report that the Peacekeepers had broken the attack on them and were now moving on into Johannesburg. In fact, she smiled, which frightened him even more. An immediate execution was something the man could have understood; that was the usual punishment for anyone who brought Madame Jumal bad news. Her smile was usually reserved for those who were to die a more prolonged death. This time, though, apparently his leader's smile meant something else entirely.

"Let them come on into the city," she said, her white teeth bared between bright red lips as she turned to the map and plotted the route of the Peacekeeper column. "My brave Simbas couldn't face their helicopter gunships and died like men. But the missiles at the stadium will keep their gunships at bay."

She turned back to the officer. "Order the Impis to gather in Johannesburg and to prepare themselves for an assault on the stadium. Tell them, though, to keep well away from these Americans. Let them join their white brothers at the stadium, and then we will kill them all in the same place."

The Simba saluted and left the command center as fast as he could go.

THREE HOURS LATER, the outskirts of Jo'burg were deserted as Echo Company cautiously made their way toward the sports stadium on the southeastern edge of the town. By now the harsh African sun was directly overhead, and the grunts welcomed the slower pace. They had been pushing hard all morning and could use the breather before they reached the stadium and went into the attack.

The Tilt Wings that had flown Rosemont and Sullivan's First Platoon in to reinforce Stuart's battered unit had evacuated the Peacekeeper dead and wounded back to the airfield. Even though they had been outnumbered more than five to one, Second Platoon had taken relatively few casualties. Only three were dead and another seven wounded. But, considering that they had been on the ground only half a day, when Stuart's casualties were added to the three grunts who had been wounded during the assault on the airstrip, the butcher's bill was starting to mount up.

The two teams from Ashley Wells's recon platoon were up on the point of the formation scouting the way through the maze of small shacks and houses. This time, however, Rosemont wasn't up with the recon teams. Usually he preferred to be with his lead elements, commanding the action from the point of contact, but this operation was too critical for him to risk being cut off from the rest of the company if recon suddenly stepped in it. So, instead of being up with Kat's Strider Alpha team, he was half a kilometer behind with the lead elements of Mick Sullivan's First Platoon. Jeb Stuart's Second Platoon was another half klick behind them in position to move to reinforce in any direction.

Although Rosemont wasn't up with the recon grunts, this didn't mean that he was operating blind. He was comlinked to them, and the display on the inside of his helmet visor fed him the same data they were picking up through their imagers and sensors. So far, there had been no signs of the hostile forces. In fact, they had seen few signs of anyone at all. What should have been teeming suburbs on the outskirts of the city were deserted. There were no trails of smoke rising from family cook fires, no children playing in the dusty streets and alleys and no women shopping in the markets and stalls.

Even deeper into the edge of the city, the small shops were all shuttered and locked. The streets were littered with trash and completely deserted. Once a prosperous city of more than two million people, Johannesburg looked as if the hand of death had passed over it.

Regardless, the Peacekeepers didn't relax their vigilance. If anything, the deserted streets made them even more cautious. One of the few things that could make people completely abandon their homes and livelihoods was the presence of troops, in this case, the dreaded Simbas. After seeing them in action, Rosemont had no desire to stumble into an ambush in this clustered, built-up area. If he had to fight the Simbas again, he wanted them out on open ground where he could see them.

"Bold Lancer, Strider." Ashley's voice cut in on his earphones. Ashley's recon teams were well out in front of the main body now, carefully checking the approach route one building at a time. "Strider Alpha's got the stadium in sight. She says it's only guarded with a light force, not much more than a reinforced platoon, and she doesn't see anything in heavy weapons."

"Affirm," Rosemont sent back. That was the Intel they had gotten from the Bat overflights, but it was nice to have the information confirmed. "Get all their locations marked, and as soon as we join up with you, we'll go into the assault."

"Strider, affirm."

Now that they had contact, First Platoon moved into an assault formation and Second Platoon moved up close behind them to support the attack. From back inside the line of buildings facing the side of the stadium, Rosemont could clearly see their objective. The stadium was formidable and a perfect defensive position, but based on what the Bats had shown and Kat's recon team had confirmed, the hostiles weren't using it to their best advantage. That was bad for them and good for Echo Company.

As soon as he saw that the assault teams were in position, Rosemont flashed the order to go. The firefight was brief. With Second Platoon providing covering fire, the First Platoon grunts assaulted the Simba guards, cutting them down before they even had a chance to defend themselves. No quarter was asked and none given. Rosemont had enough to deal with without the problem of handling POWs.

As soon as the last shot was fired, he sent Stuart to take out the missile launchers and moved First Platoon into the stadium.

THE PLAYING FIELD of the People's Sports Stadium was crowded to overflowing. Men, women and children of all ages took up almost every square foot of ground. They shrank from the Peacekeepers until Rosemont slid his helmet visor up and they saw his white skin. Then they swarmed all over their rescuers.

"Who's in charge here?" Rosemont called out in English, his voice amplified by the small speakers built into his command helmet comlink.

A middle-aged man wearing a dirty tropical suit coat worked his way through the crowd. "It very well may be that I am," the man said, glancing around to see if anyone would question his authority. "Ian Browning, late of Kroonstad."

"Major Alexander Rosemont," Rosemont said, extending his hand. "United States Expeditionary Force. We're here to take you people to safety."

"If you're planing to fly us out, Major," Browning said tensely, "I think I should warn you that the stadium's surrounded by antiaircraft missiles. I saw them being set up when they brought me in."

"We know about them," Rosemont replied. "And we're taking care of them right now."

As if to lend authority to his words, a massive explosion rocked the stadium, and a column of greasy black smoke rose up into the sky.

"That's the first of the launching sites going up now. As soon as we've taken them all out, I'll get the aircraft in here and start the evacuation. We're taking you to an airstrip at Malaika, and you'll be flown to safety from there. You should be out of the country by midnight."

Browning smiled for the first time.

"How many people do you have in here?" Rosemont asked.

"We really haven't had time to take an accurate count," Browning admitted. "But I would say that there are at least six hundred of us all told."

Rosemont grimaced. The briefing had said that he could expect two to three hundred hostages at the most. This was looking worse and worse all the time.

"Madame Jumal's been arresting every white she can find anywhere near the city," Browning explained. "New people have been coming in almost every hour for the last three days. We have quite a few wounded among us and, while we have had water, none of us has been fed since we arrived."

"We have field rations with us," Rosemont said. "But we're traveling light and probably have only about thirty or forty meals. We won't be able to feed everyone until we get you to the airstrip, but you're welcome to what rations we have with us."

"Thank you, Major," Browning said. "I'll see that the food goes to the children and the injured first."

Rosemont quickly flashed orders to Sullivan for the platoon medics to set up an aid station and start treating the wounded hostages. Even though he saw that the grunts were handing out rations on their own, he also told Sullivan to set up a ration distribution point.

The explosion of another missile launcher echoed through the stadium, and Rosemont checked his comlink. If Stuart kept going at this pace, they should be ready to start the evacuation in another hour.

"Get your people organized as fast as you can," he told Browning. "With this many people, we're short of aircraft. The women with children, the elderly, the sick and the injured will go out first. The men and the able-bodied younger women will wait till later flights."

"We also have some blacks with us," Browning said. "Will you take them, too?"

Rosemont looked at Browning as if he had two heads. Even though apartheid had ended more than thirty years previously, apparently the specter of segregation was still alive in the Bantu People's Democracy. "Of course," he said. "Everyone who is in danger goes."

Browning looked relieved. "Good, I'll pass the word."

Simba Command Center, Pretoria, August 12

The Simba commo officer rushed into Madame Jumal's operations room with the message that the Americans had reached the stadium in Johannesburg and had overwhelmed the small Simba unit guarding the hostages.

"Good." Madame Jewel Jumal smiled as she studied the large-scale map of the city. "Now I have them exactly where I want them."

She turned to the Simba officer awaiting her next order. "Order the attack," she said. "And tell the Impis to let none escape. I want them all dead this time."

He raised his clenched fist in salute.

Jumal turned back to her map. She repressed a shiver of excitement when she thought of dead Peacekeepers. With this one stroke she would become the most powerful national leader in all of Africa. No one would ever question her strength or determination again. The other African rulers would come to her on their knees, begging her advice and wisdom. She would be the greatest woman in African history.

THE RECON TEAM with Stuart's missile-hunting Second Platoon were the first to spot the Simbas when they moved into the far end of the huge public square in front of the stadium. They flashed an alert to Stuart, who instantly passed it on to Rosemont. The company commander was going over the evacuation procedures with Mick Sullivan when his comlink beeped. "Lancer, go."

"Lancer," Stuart called. "Cowboy, we've got company. There's at least a battalion of Simbas headed our way."

"Pull back inside the stadium, Cowboy," Rosemont answered. "And bring Strider in with you."

"There's still a couple of those missile launchers we haven't gotten around to yet, Lancer."

"Leave 'em. We'll deal with 'em later."

"Cowboy, affirm."

As Sullivan dashed off to rejoin his platoon, Rosemont found Browning at the makeshift aid station where the medics were treating the injured hostages.

"Tell your people to take cover in the bleachers," he told the hostage leader. "There's a large hostile force moving into position at the other end of the square, and I think they're going to try to take us out."

"Is there anything we can do to help your men, Major?" Browning asked.

"Have any of your people had military training?"

"I have, Major, with the Kroonstad Defense Battalion," Browning replied with a touch of pride. "And I'm sure there are several dozen more veterans."

"Get them together and arm yourselves with the weapons and ammunition from the dead Simbas. I'll give you an NCO who will have a comlink to me. Follow his orders."

"What do you want us to do?"

"I want you to stay with the others and guard them in case anyone slips past us."

"But we want to fight."

"I know you do," Rosemont said impatiently. "But this is not a game we're playing here. This is a job for professionals. You'll have enough to do backing us up and protecting your noncombatants."

"Yes sir," Browning reluctantly agreed, and went to organize his hostage militia.

WITH SECOND PLATOON and the recon team closing in on the stadium, Rosemont hurried to plan his defense. The People's Sports Stadium couldn't have been a better place for him to defend if he had built it himself. Circular in shape, its concrete outer walls were terraced in three levels and were broken with only four entrances. Each entrance had a stout gate, and the terraces had concrete balustrades high enough to serve as cover for the defenders against anything except tank or direct artillery fire.

With both platoons and the two recon teams, he had more than enough grunts to hold the place against an infantry assault for weeks. As long as their ammunition held out, that is.

On the minus side, though, he had nothing in the line of heavy weapons. Since he had wanted to move fast, he had left his heavy weaponry behind to guard the airfield. Normally he would have them airlifted, but since all of the antiaircraft missile sites had not been taken out yet, he couldn't risk trying it. As long as the Simbas didn't bring up tanks or their gunships, though, he should be okay with just the small arms. But if they did, Echo Company would be in serious trouble.

After checking the disposition of his troops, Rosemont got on the comlink back to the airfield to appraise Hansen of the situation at the stadium. The aviation officer listened grimly as Rosemont spelled out his situation.

"I can send you some Bull Pups," he said, referring to the shoulder-fired, bunker-busting, ground-assault missiles in the Peacekeepers' arsenal. "And have them on the ground in half an hour."

"No," Rosemont said. "I don't want to risk the aircraft. We have about six hundred people to get out of here, and we're going to need every ship we have. As it is, I'll even have to use the Bubble Tops to ferry some of them out if we want to get this done before dark."

"I can try to send the Bull Pups in on the Bats," Hansen said, desperate to find a way to help his commander.

"Better save 'em in case we need more small-arms ammunition," Rosemont replied. "We only have our basic combat load with us, and I think we're going to burn through that pretty quick."

"I'll pull the sensor package out of one of the Bats right now," Hansen said. "Load it with 5 mm and have it standing by on the launcher for you."

"Good idea."

"Major." Sullivan's voice broke in over Rosemont's comlink. "I'm on the top of the main gate and

I think you'd better come up here and take a look at this. We've got us a bigger problem than we thought."

Rosemont frowned. Now what in the hell had gone wrong?

"On the way."

THE MAIN GATE of the stadium was crested with twin towers like a medieval fortress. The walkway stretching between the base of the towers was crowned with a crenellated battlement, which heightened the resemblance to a fortress. It was a perfect place to observe the approach to the stadium, and Rosemont didn't even have to use his imager to see what was wrong. The broad boulevard leading up to the main gate was filled to overflowing with howling Simbas. As he watched, even more of them poured in from the side streets. What had been originally reported as a battalion of Simbas now looked like at least two thousand of them, and more were coming in every minute.

"This reminds me of the Alamo," Sullivan said, eyeing the packed ranks. "We're in the fort, and all the hostiles in the world are swarming around us right outside of small-arms range. The only thing we're missing is a fat guy with one leg on horseback directing the mob and a Mexican playing a trumpet."

"Speaking of the Alamo," Jeb commented, "we could sure as hell use some horse artillery right about now to ride around on their flank and tear them a new asshole."

"We could use some artillery, period," Sullivan said. "I'd even settle for one of those old muzzle loaders Colonel Travis had at the Alamo."

Rosemont smiled. "You gentlemen have just given me a great idea. I think I can get us some artillery, at least one tube's worth."

He keyed his mike implant. "Hook Talon, Lancer."

"Talon," Hansen instantly replied.

"Lancer. There is something you can do to help us."

"Send it."

BACK AT THE AIRFIELD, Hank Rivera's gunners quickly broke down one of their rocket mortars and loaded it into a Tilt Wing that already had her turbines spooled up and her rotors spinning. When the gunners had the weapon tied down, the support people passed crates of rocket ammunition into the aircraft and lashed them down around the disassembled tube. As soon as the last crate was loaded, Rivera and the gun crew clambered on board. The Tilt Wing lifted off in a flurry of dust and headed in the direction of Jo'burg as fast as her screaming turbines could carry her.

A little more than halfway to the city, Rivera spotted a small hill standing clear of the surrounding brush and directed the pilot to land on top of it. The hill was at the extreme range for the rocket mortar, but it was easily defendable and looked to be miles from any hostile activity. "Down there," he told the pilot.

Before the aircraft's rotors had even stopped turning, the gunners had the rear ramp down and were unloading the mortar and ammunition. While the gun crew assembled the mortar and loaded the ammo feed tray with the 120 mm rocket projectiles, Rivera set up the FDC monitor and linked to the main fire computer back at the airstrip.

"We're up," the gun captain told Rivera.

"Bold Lancer," Rivera flashed to Rosemont. "Bold Thunder Xray. We are in position, locked and loaded."

"Lancer, affirm. Flashing defcons now."

The DFC monitor screen lit up with the defensive concentrations Rosemont had plotted. Though they ringed the stadium, he had plotted several extra shots in the square facing the main gate.

"Thunder Xray, confirm defcon one through eight."

"Lancer, affirm. Fire by number on my command."

"Thunder Xray, standing by."

NO SOONER HAD Rosemont flashed his defcons than there was a stirring in the front of the packed Simba ranks. "Here they come!" Sullivan sent.

"Let 'em come," Rosemont said calmly. "I don't want 'em to scatter into the buildings."

The Simbas started firing long before they were within effective range. As per Rosemont's orders, most of the grunts held their fire. The unit's snipers, however, had fixed their scopes on their LARs and were delivering well-aimed shots at selected targets.

Seated behind a concrete balustrade on the top of the main gate, Ironstone took his time as he picked his targets on the other side of the square. Any time he saw a Simba who looked as if he was giving orders, he focused in on him and put a bullet through his head. So far, he had zeroed half a dozen Simba leaders, and it looked as if he was getting results in his sector. Without their officers and NCOs driving them into the face of the Peacekeepers' fire, the Simba troops seemed a little more reluctant to step forward and die.

Several overly enthusiastic individuals had run on ahead of the pack, however, and were closing in on the stadium. To keep them from getting in too close, the Indian marksman switched to firing on them. A half-dozen quick shots hit as many men, and most of them stayed down.

Rosemont patiently waited until the Simbas were fully committed to the assault before he called for the defcons. He wanted them massed in the open square where Rivera's mortar rounds could do the most damage to them. When it looked as if he had all the targets he could handle, he keyed his mike implant. "Thunder Xray, Bold Lancer."

"Thunder Xray, go."

"Fire defcons three, five and six. Three rounds, Fire-cracker, midburst. Internal guidance."

"Thunder Xray, affirm. On the way."

Less than a minute later the first rocket round detonated in the air over the middle of the square. A bursting charge in the Firecracker warhead split it open, and a dozen submunition canisters blew out in a circular pattern. Each canister contained its own EHE bursting charge surrounded by dozens of triangular-shaped, tempered-steel pellets embedded in a foam matrix. When the canisters detonated a millisecond later, the pellets were propelled downward with the force of a machine gun bullet.

The effect on the Simbas was as if they had been caught in a storm of hardened steel hailstones flying faster than the speed of sound. The pellets could punch through light armored vehicles, and the Simbas' camouflaged field uniforms didn't slow them down at all.

In their battle frenzy, the Simbas didn't seem to realize what was killing them at first. By now they were halfway across the square, and the detonations of the rocket warheads weren't noticeable over the roar of the small-arms fire going both ways. More rounds followed, each leaving a small black puff of smoke in the sky from the bursting charges and a dozen smaller white puffs when the submunitions EHE charges went off.

Even with the carnage, the Simbas were still pressing the attack and the grunts were taking casualties. It was time to go to the final option. "Thunder Xray," Rosemont flashed. "Lancer."

"Xray, go."

"Fire defcons one and two. Four rounds, Firecracker, low burst, danger close."

"Xray, affirm danger close. Keep your heads down, Lancer."

"That's most affirm."

Rosemont sounded the danger-close-artillery warning over the comlink and the grunts took cover. Such warnings were called for when the rounds were coming in less that fifty meters in front of the friendly forces. Since the Firecracker warheads had a fifty-meter bursting radius, some of the deadly pellets would be falling on Echo Company.

This time the Firecracker rounds were clearly heard over the rattle of small-arms fire. Set for low burst, they were detonating only a hundred meters above the ground. At that height, the pellets didn't have time to fully disperse. Where one pellet had struck before, now three did. Each detonating round added to the destruction, and the Simbas finally broke and ran.

When the last detonation echoed away, Rosemont rose and looked out over the approach to the stadium. The broad boulevard leading to the main gate was littered with the bloody carnage of war. Rivera's Firecracker warheads had done terrible damage to the massed Simbas. Torn bodies were stacked three deep in some places. The moans and cries of the wounded reached them like a muted roar. Men crawled away as fast as they could, leaving trails of bright red behind them.

Normally Rosemont would have sent his medics to aid the hostile wounded, but not this time. He knew that there were more where they had come from, and he wasn't going to further risk his people. Hopefully it would be a while before they could get organized again to mount another assault, and by that time he should be able to get the bulk of the hostages flown out.

Sullivan reported to Rosemont. "It looks like it's over for now," he said. "They've completely pulled back."

Rosemont called Rivera. "Cease fire on defcons. I'm flashing new targets."

This time he sent the positions of the remaining missile launchers to the FDC. With the remnants of the Simbas out there, he didn't want to risk his grunts by sending them out to destroy the launchers. "Expend remaining rounds on these targets," he ordered.

This time the explosions sounded loud as the EHE warheads found the missile launchers. Secondary explosions followed as the missile propellants detonated, and greasy black smoke boiled up into the sky.

"Lancer," Rivera called. "Thunder Xray. We've run dry and we're heading back to the barn."

"Good shooting, Thunder. Thanks."

"*De nada,* Lancer. Good luck."

8

East of Johannesburg, August 12

Jan Rikermann's army of Boer exiles moved steadily through the wooded coastal plains east of Johannesburg. Most of the thousand men were on foot, clearing both sides of the road they traveled to protect the motorized transport with their heavy weapons, ammunition and supplies. They moved slowly, but out in the open, confident that they wouldn't be spotted by the deep-space recon satellites. They could display that confidence because a Boer sympathizer at EuroSpaceCom had given Rikermann the IFF codes that would tell the satellite they were an International Red Cross relief column. The IFF codes couldn't protect them from recon aircraft, but the French-made Rapier antiaircraft missiles they carried would.

Dov Merov was back with the trucks transporting his ground-to-ground ballistic missiles when he received the word that Rikermann wanted to see him. The Israeli weapons designer found the Boer leader at the head of the column in his command vehicle, an ex-Israeli army armored skimmer. "You wanted to see me, Jan?"

"Yes, Dov, I have news," Rikermann announced. "Apparently the Americans have dealt themselves into this situation. They have landed a small Peacekeeper force and are trying to evacuate Madame Jumal's white hostages from Johannesburg. The Simbas are gathering to stop them, but I don't think they will succeed. The danger is, of course, that the Americans might learn of us when they are hunting for the Simbas."

"Do you think they would try to oppose us if they discovered us?" Merov asked.

"No." Rikermann's faded blue eyes took on the look of biblical prophet as he shook his white-haired head. "I think not, Dov. There are too few of them, and their only mission here is to free the whites. When that is accomplished, their orders are for them to withdraw. If all goes as they have planned, they will be gone by early tomorrow morning."

Dov didn't bother to ask how Rikermann knew the Peacekeepers' battle plans. The Boer leader had more eyes in Africa than he could possibly count and obviously he had a pipeline into the United States, as well. This didn't surprise the Israeli, though. Time and again Rikermann's Intelligence organization had proven to be one of the most efficient in the world. But then it had to have been in order for his plans to have come this far.

When the white minority government of what had once been the nation of South Africa fell in 2008, not all of the white population capitulated to the new regime. In fact, many of them did not. The majority of the hard-core white holdouts had been Boers, the descendants of the original Dutch settlers who had tamed an African wilderness in the seventeenth century and built the nation that later became known as South Africa.

Fearing that they would suffer the fate of the whites who had remained in Rhodesia when it became Zimbabwe and converted to black rule in 1980, the Boers abandoned their ancestral lands and fled the new black-governed nation. Determined to leave the country as they had found it three hundred years before, they burned their farms and businesses before they left. More importantly, though, they destroyed the gold and diamond mines that had been a major source of South Africa's wealth for so many years. If they couldn't enjoy the fruits of their labors, then no one else would, either.

Fleeing with what they could carry on their backs, some of the Boers went back to a cold reception in Holland. Though they were originally descended from Dutch farmers, they had been away from their mother country too long to fit into twenty-first-century European society. Some of them fled to farms in the northern reaches of western Canada and tried to learn to live in that much colder climate.

The majority of the exiles, however, settled in the undeveloped areas of Argentina. In the final years of the white government, the South Africans and the Argentines had become firm allies, drawn together by sharing advanced technology. The Argentines welcomed the Boers and the wealth they brought both in the form of smuggled diamonds and in their ethic of hard work.

Jan Rikermann had been a young man when he fled to Argentina, a young man with a burning desire for revenge on those who had forced his people out of their homeland. Though he was young, he quickly established a clandestine government in exile and started planning to retake their nation. Using the underground networks left over from the previous century when the Nazis fled the fall of the Third Reich and settled in Argentina, he first secured a sound financial base with the diamonds that had been smuggled out of South Africa.

The destruction of the mines had caused chaos in the diamond market, driving up the price of the gems. Having come from one of the large diamond families, Rikermann invested their stones well. So well, in fact, that the proceeds allowed the Boers to buy large tracts of land, and they quickly became prosperous farmers and ranchers again. Once their finances were secured, Rikermann further copied the methods that had been used by the earlier Nazi exiles. The Boers dug in on their new lands, isolated themselves from prying eyes and worked to prepare for the day when they could return to their lost homeland.

Over the years Rikermann hadn't allowed his dream to die. Using a mixture of racial pride, religion and rigid military discipline, he forged the exiles into an organization not unlike the Nazi party. Unlike the Nazis, however, who had planned and plotted to no avail, the Boer's dream was now being fulfilled. They were back in their South Africa with a powerful army, and the days of the black government were numbered.

After years of planning and struggle, the last of the pieces were finally in place and the operation could begin. When it was over, the Bantu People's Democracy would be the Republic of South Africa once again, and it would be the home of the Boer people who had created it from the African wilderness in the first place. The only thing that could possibly stop them now was the Peacekeepers.

Rikermann seemed to be totally unconcerned about the Americans, however, and that bothered Merov. Being an Israeli, he'd had a ringside seat to their recent operation in the Middle East and he knew what they could do when they went into action. "I hope you're right about the Peacekeepers," he said. "But I know they aren't like the UN troops."

"If the Americans decide to interfere with us—" the Boer shrugged "—we can deal with them, too—never fear, Dov. We are home now and we will stay. And remember, it is your home now, too."

Merov had no doubt that the weapons in the convoy they guarded would kill Americans as well as they would kill blacks. He had designed the neutron warheads for the missiles himself and he knew their effectiveness. Unlike other nuclear weapons, neutron warheads didn't kill by blast and fire, but by an intense burst of short-lived, hard radiation. The radiation killed all higher life, but left structures and the land completely untouched. The technology needed to make these deadly weapons wasn't simple, but it had been known since the 1970s.

The fact that they killed bloodlessly, and did so without damaging property, had made them anathema to the great nuclear powers of the Cold War. In fact, even during the height of the Cold War, both the Soviets and the Americans had made a pact not to build such devices. Even then the thought of war without blood was unthinkable, not to mention the idea that human beings would be exterminated while the material things of the world would be left undamaged. For Rikermann's plan, however, the neutron warheads were essential. They would kill the population, but would leave the country intact.

Merov had reconciled himself to killing the blacks who ruled the Bantu People's Democracy so his people would have a place to live. The question was did he want to be responsible for killing American Peacekeepers? Being an Israeli citizen, Merov knew the Americans as his nation's best friends and allies. Had it not been for the United States, his parents would have never gotten out of the Soviet Union. Even though the fate of thousands of his own people hung on the success of the Boer's mission, it was difficult for him to see the Peacekeepers as his enemies.

ROSEMONT TOOK one last look at the blood-soaked square in front of the stadium before getting back to the task at hand. "Okay," he told Sullivan. "Let's start getting the hostages ready. I want them to start loading the instant the first ship touches down. Also I want our casualties to go out on the first load, as well."

"Yes, sir," the XO answered.

"And," Rosemont added, "when you call for the lift, tell Hansen to bring the cargo slings with the ships. I want you and your people to go back in a sling load."

"Sir?"

Rosemont grinned. Riding a cargo sling under a Tilt Wing was an unorthodox way to travel, but it could be done. "I need you to go back and take command of the airfield as soon as possible so you can run the evacuation from that end. Since there are more hostages here than we were told, I can't spare the aircraft to fly you. Also I want you back there in case the Simbas try the airfield again. I think we're safe here for a while. But even if we're not, I can hold them off with Second Platoon and a little more help from Bold Thunder."

"Will do, sir."

"I'll be with Browning if you need me."

"Yes, sir."

Rosemont found Browning with his ragtag militia in front of the stadium gathering weapons and ammunition from the fallen Simbas to arm even more of his people. There was no shortage of weapons now, and some of the militia were carrying an extra rifle slung over their shoulders, as well as several bandoliers of ammunition.

"The Tilt Wings are inbound," he told the hostage leader. "As soon as they touch down, I want your people ready to board immediately. As I said before, I want the women, children and the most seriously injured to go out first."

"We'll be ready, Major," Browning said, buckling a captured Simba officer's field belt with a holstered pistol around his waist.

Rosemont next went to his aid station to check in on his wounded. He'd seen the casualty report already and knew that they were minor, mostly frag wounds from the Firecracker rounds. He did have two dead, though, one from Sullivan's platoon and one from the recon platoon. With that much lead flying around, it had to connect with someone every now and then.

He found Ashley Wells already there, and the look on her face told him why she was there. If Ashley had any major shortcoming as a combat leader, it was that she let her casualties get too far under her skin. A good leader was always concerned about the welfare of his people, but she took each wound they suffered as a personal injury to herself.

"How are your people?" he asked her.

"One dead," she snapped. "And two minor wounds."

"I'll have them flown out in the first load."

Ashley looked as if she was about to say something more, but she didn't. She had seen the condition of the hostages and knew that her casualties had not been in vain.

Just then Rosemont's comlink beeped. "Bold Lancer, Hook Talon Lead," the Bubble Top flight leader escorting the Tilt Wing transport reported. "We're inbound to your location with Talon Lift One, echo tango alpha zero two."

"Lancer, affirm. Come on in, Talon, we're ready to start loading them out."

While the two Bubble Tops orbited overhead, the Tilt Wing assault transport transitioned to vertical flight over the stadium and slowly sank down onto the cleared playing field. Leaving its turbines spinning, the transport dropped its rear ramp and the crew chief waved to the waiting stretcher-bearers. The first people to be loaded on board were Rosemont's wounded and the most seriously injured of the hostages. The balance of the load was made up with hostage women and the younger children.

Even though most of the hostages had few belongings, Rosemont had restricted them to taking only what little they could put in their pockets. All their suitcases and boxes full of family treasures had to be left behind. If possible, he would send them out in a sling load later. He did, however, let the children carry their toys on board. Rosemont was hard-core when it came to military realities, but not that hard. The children had been through enough the past couple of days, and he wasn't going to take away the small comfort of a favorite doll or teddy bear.

As soon as the hostages and Rosemont's wounded were loaded into the aircraft, the Tilt Wing rose to a hover twenty feet above the ground. A cable was lowered from the ship's belly, and two squads of First Platoon laid out the cargo net on the ground under the ship. As soon as the net was deployed and hooked up, the men and women of First Platoon crowded into it. The grunts clipped the D-rings on their assault harnesses to the netting, hooked their boots into the ropes and held on with both hands. It would be a breezy ride, but it was the only way that Rosemont could get them back to the airfield and still evacuate the hostages at the same time. When the last man was hooked up, Sullivan gave the pilot the go-ahead, and the aircraft rose, lifting the cargo net full of grunts off the ground.

"I think some of our men could go out that way," Browning said as he watched the Tilt Wing rise into the air.

Rosemont shook his head. "They don't have assault harnesses to hook onto the netting," he said. "So I wouldn't want to risk them. Believe me, it's all too easy to fall out of the damned thing."

Browning had to agree when he saw one of the grunts slip and stick both legs through the netting before his safety line caught him and kept him from falling all the way out. "You may have a point there, Major."

As the loaded Tilt Wing flew out of sight, one of the Bubble Tops broke off from its protective orbit and escorted it back. The second Tilt Wing dropped down over the stadium, and the process was repeated.

"WE'RE LOADED," the Tilt Wing pilot called over to acting load master, Jeb Stuart. When Sullivan flew back to the airstrip, Stuart inherited his job.

"Move 'em out."

With a flurry of dust from the rotors, the Tilt Wing lifted off in the hover mode. Rotating her wings as she transitioned to level flight, the ship turned to the northeast and accelerated as it climbed for altitude.

"How many is that now?" Rosemont asked Stuart.

Jeb consulted his data pad. "I've got four hundred and eighty-six, which leaves us only a hundred and seventy-two left to go, sir."

By making the hostages stand in the cargo bay of the Tilt Wings instead of sitting in the jump seats, they had been able to load three times as many people as the aircraft was designed to carry. The extra weight wasn't a problem, because a Tilt Wing was powerful enough to lift twice the weight of a load of hostages, but its internal space was limited. They were even having people stand in the small space behind the pilot's seat to crowd a few more onto each flight.

"We're not moving 'em out fast enough," Rosemont said, his eyes taking in the low angle of the setting sun. "We're going to lose the light in another half hour."

"I guess we'll just have to continue after dark, sir." Stuart did a quick calculation. "I read that three more flights should get the last of them."

Considering the larger number of hostages he had had to deal with, and the little interruption caused by the Simbas, Rosemont had to admit that the airlift had gone as well as could have been expected. Had Force Intel known more about the true situation ahead of time, they could have sent more evacuation aircraft. But even with so few planes, it was still going well. "Which will still leave us here," the company commander pointed out.

"Shit, sir." Stuart shook his head. "I'm sorry. I completely forgot all about us. That's one more flight if we can get both Bubble Tops to come in and pick up the recon teams."

Rosemont laughed. After having fought three battles in less than twelve hours and having evacuated twice as many hostages as they had expected, it was understandable if the platoon leader had lost track of one minor detail.

"Don't sweat the small stuff, LT," he said. "We're grunts, we can always walk out."

"Jesus, sir. I sure hope not."

9

Pretoria, August 12

Madame Jewel Jumal was so angry that she almost hissed. Her earlier good mood had instantly evaporated when word had come of the defeat of the Simba Impis at the stadium. The fact that most of the officers responsible for the failure were dead in the carnage at the square had done nothing to appease her anger at their defeat. It had made her look bad, and Jumal had no tolerance for anything that made her look bad.

Worse than that, though, was the fact that the white hostages were getting away from her. The key to consolidating her power was to have someone to blame for the crisis that had brought her to power. Without the hostages to publicly punish, the people might focus on her takeover of the government, and that could cause trouble.

"Do we have no more missiles?" she asked. "Can you not shoot those airplanes down?"

"More missiles are being moved into place," one Simba said. "But it will take some time before they are ready to fire."

"But they will get away," she said. "I cannot have that."

"Madame," another Simba officer ventured. "There is a way to regain our honor. Even though the whites have been flown out of the stadium, they aren't out of the country yet. We can still attack the airfield and kill them there. Also the Peacekeepers are still at the stadium, and when night falls we can attack them there, too."

That was what Jumal had wanted to hear, a way to salvage something from this humiliation. She would never gain the political stature she sought if the hostages or the Americans escaped alive. In fact, it would make her a laughingstock in Africa. And no one laughed at Madame Jewel Jumal.

"You will do both," she snapped. "I want both the whites and the Americans dead."

The Simba answered with a clenched-fist salute.

THE SOFT AFRICAN NIGHT was falling over the national sports stadium. While the grunts kept watch from the second tier of the outer wall, Rosemont and Stuart were down on the playing field waiting for the next lift ship to come in. So far, the airlift had gone like clockwork. From the reports Sullivan was sending from the airstrip, the STOL transports were also coming in on time and evacuating the freed hostages to the refugee camp that had been set up for them in Morocco. Two more flights into the stadium and it would be over. Then Echo Company would pull back to the airstrip and prepare to evacuate themselves. If all went well, they'd be out of the country by midnight.

Rosemont was pleased that the mission was closing as quickly as it was. Even now that the situation seemed to be well under control, this wasn't the kind of operation the Peacekeepers had been designed to perform. This rescue should have been handled by UN troops, or the UN eunuchs, as his grunts called them. But as usual, the UN had been unable to move fast enough to save their lives and had called on the USEF. He was proud of the job Echo Company had done, but he still wanted them back home at Fort Benning as soon as possible.

"The next one should be here any minute, sir," Stuart said, glancing at his data pad.

Just then the voice of the Tilt Wing pilot came in over Rosemont's earphones. "Bold Lancer, Talon Lift Two."

"Lancer, go."

"Lift Two. I'm getting missile radar readouts and am taking evasive action at this time. I'm sorry, Lancer, but I've got to get the hell out of the area."

"Affirm, Lift. Good luck."

Rosemont swore under his breath. He had been afraid that the Simbas would get their shit together and do something like this. It had been too much to hope that they would leave them alone long enough to get away clean. He looked around the darkening stadium for Browning and saw that the hostage leader was with a group of his militia by the main gate. "Flash it to your people," he told Stuart, "while I tell Browning the good news."

"Yes, sir."

Browning apparently was expecting more good news and greeted Rosemont enthusiastically. "I say, Major, we'll be home in time for dinner, right?"

"I'm afraid not," Rosemont said bluntly. "We've had another hang-up. The Tilt Wing reported that the Simbas have moved more antiaircraft missiles into the city. We've got to stop the airlift until we can get the Bats back in to locate the launchers and we can take them out."

"How long do you think that will take?"

Rosemont shrugged. "I have no idea. Now that we've lost the element of surprise, that depends entirely on the Simbas. All they have to do to hold us up here is to keep the mobile launchers on the move. Or they can use them as bait to suck us into an ambush. I'm afraid that they're holding all the good cards this time."

"Damn!" Browning looked grim. "That means they have us trapped here."

Not yet, the company commander thought. There was still one joker he could play. "Mr. Browning, do you think your people would be willing to try to get out of here tonight on foot?"

Browning didn't have to think about it for more than a brief moment. "I don't see why not, Major," he answered. "We have our women and children out, and we don't mind taking the risk ourselves. Anything is better than waiting here for the Simbas to come back."

"Okay, talk to your people and get back to me ASAP. Also I'll need an exact head count of all who are left."

"I'll get right on it, Major."

When the final count was done, Browning reported that only forty-seven hostages were left, and all of them were either able-bodied men or teenage boys. A straw poll had been taken, and they were all for trying to get out tonight rather than waiting the night out.

It took some time to prepare the ex-hostages for the march. Stripping the hostile dead provided them with needed clothing, shoes and, most of all, weapons and field equipment. By the time they were done, everyone who wanted a weapon had one and almost everyone had a jacket and a full canteen, as well. It would be a hungry march, though. All of Echo Company's rations had gone to feed the hungry hostages, and the hostile dead had not been carrying field rations.

But if they could get out of Jo'burg safely tonight, a growling stomach would be a small price to pay for their freedom.

WHILE THE EX-HOSTAGES were equipping themselves, Rosemont got on the comlink to go over his new plan with Sullivan. The XO wasn't happy about the idea of their trying to walk out, but there was little he could do about it. He had his hands full coordinating the evacuation, and all of his troops were needed to secure the airstrip. The Simbas knew where they were and what they were doing, and there was always a chance that they would attack again.

While he couldn't send troops, he could get a Bat in the air and keep a pair of armed Bubble Tops on ramp alert to provide air support once they got out of range of the missiles. It wasn't much, but it made him feel a little better about the situation.

It was almost ten o'clock before Rosemont finally had all his people formed up in the stadium ready to move out. Kat Wallenska's Strider Alpha team was up on point, followed by the bulk of Second Platoon. The mass of hostages would go in the middle of the formation, with the Strider Bravo recon team bringing up the rear.

Before he ordered the advance, Rosemont checked in one last time with Sullivan. "Bold Racer, Lancer."

"Racer, go."

"We're ready to go."

"Racer, affirm. I'll get the Bat in the air ASAP. And as soon as you break out of the missile ring, I'll send in the Bubble Tops. Good luck, Lancer."

"Thanks," Rosemont answered. "Bold Lancer, moving out now."

The moon was not yet up when Kat's recon team slipped out of the main gate of the stadium. With their chameleon suits dialed to matt black, the grunts were invisible in the deep shadows. Quickly moving past the piles of dead Simbas in the square, they headed for a side street leading out of the city. As soon as they had taken cover in the buildings on the other side of the square, Kat flashed the go-ahead signal and the main body moved out behind them.

Unlike the recon grunts, many of the hostages could be seen in the dark. Despite taking camouflage jackets from the Simba bodies and trying to darken their light-colored clothing with mud, many of the hostages stood out in the dark as if they were carrying lanterns. Once they, too, were on the other side of the square, they took cover in the deepest shadows.

Now that everyone was out of the square, Kat took point and led her team down the narrow street. One block from the square, the street turned into an even narrower, winding alley. Another hundred meters farther on, the alley stopped. According to the map on her nav screen, they should go left, so she motioned her numbers three and four to leapfrog forward while she and Ironstone covered them. At the next bend in the alley, the two grunts stopped and Kat moved up again.

She took cover in shadow and peered through her IR imager, trying to see into the darkness. Moving through this jumbled, crowded maze of shacks and back alleys wasn't her idea of a fun time. There was too much sunbaked metal that still retained heat from the day and gave off false IR readings. The metal also threw off her MAAD detectors. For all practical purposes, her high-tech sensors and detectors were useless, and she was reduced to having to use her bare eyeballs.

And if that wasn't bad enough, she was having difficulty translating what she could see to what her nav screen map display was showing. Obviously the map was badly out of date and close to being completely useless. Kat hated to admit that she was lost, but that was a fairly accurate assessment of her situation. All she could do was take a compass reading for east and try to follow it to the edge of the built-up area.

Wherever she was, though, the area seemed to be deserted. So far, she had seen no signs of any of the people who lived here. Even though the hour was late, there should have been some sign of the teeming humanity that inhabited this maze of shacks and small shops. There was nothing, not even a stray dog or a crying baby, and that bothered her.

Crouching beside his team leader, John Ironstone checked out the area through his rifle's sniper scope. Like Kat, he was also wary of the deserted area, very wary. He knew that many Africans went to sleep with the setting sun, but that was only those who lived in the villages. In Johannesburg there should have been someone running around even this late at night. This was spooky.

"Ironman," Kat whispered. "Two o'clock, fifty meters, moving toward us."

Ironstone brought his weapon to bear with a smooth movement and quickly focused in on the furtive figure Kat had spotted. Even though it was keeping to the deepest shadows, he could plainly see through the light intensifying scope that the figure was male. He could also see that whoever they were stalking wasn't armed, and he held his fire.

"He's not packin'," he informed Kat. "Grab his ass and see where he's going."

"Affirm. Cover me."

Moving like her feline namesake, Kat slipped out of the shadows and quickly crossed the narrow street. As Ironstone kept the target in his sights, he saw Kat move into his scope's field of vision. A flash of movement, and she had the man on his back on the ground, her knife at his throat.

"Shit! He's just a kid," she informed the Indian as she pulled her knife back and jerked him to his feet.

"Bring him back anyway," Ironstone said. "Maybe he can tell us what's going on around here."

As recon's language expert, Ironstone had received a full hypno implant on the Afrikaans language on the flight over. He just hoped that this kid spoke the Boer language, because he sure as hell didn't know a word of Bantu.

"Who are you?" he asked in Afrikaans.

To his relief, the boy answered in the same language.

"What'd he say?" Kat whispered.

"He says his name's Robert Motobu, and he's a student at Saint Anthony's school."

"What's he doing out so late at night?"

"He says he was looking for us so he could warn us that there's a big group of Simbas a few hundred meters up the road waiting for us. He says they have machine guns and other heavy weapons with them."

"How did he know where we were?"

"He says that everyone knows we're here. They know that we're the Peacekeepers and we came to help the white people the Simbas were holding."

"That's all we fucking need," Kat muttered. "We might as well have brought the fucking regimental band. Ask him why he's telling us all this."

Leave it to Kat to stick to basics. The thought that this kid might be leading them into an ambush had crossed his mind, as well. "He says that he hates the Simbas because they killed his uncle. He also says they took his white schoolteacher, beat him up and put him in prison. He's pissed off and says he wants to do something to help."

"How can we bypass the Simbas?"

Ironstone quizzed the boy further.

"He says there's a way through this alley that can take us past them. He says he can guide us and bring us out on the other side of their position."

"Do you think we can trust him?"

The Indian shrugged in the darkness. "Damned if I know, but he's all we've got to work with."

"I'd better check up on this," Kat said as she keyed her comlink.

Rosemont wasn't too sure that following a black kid through a maze of shacks and back alleys was the best command decision he had ever made in his military career. But unless he wanted to risk going head-to-head with the Simbas in a costly night battle in a built-up area, he really had no choice.

"Go ahead, Alpha," he transmitted back to Kat. "But keep a close eye on that kid. And for Christ's sake, don't let him out of your sight. Shoot the little bastard if you have to, but don't let him get away from you."

"That's most affirm, Lancer."

Johannesburg, August 13

Young Robert Motobu slipped through the maze of slum alleys as only a native resident could. Kat and Ironstone dogged his heels—Kat to try to keep him in sight, and Ironstone to try to keep him in his sights. Though the Indian wanted to trust the boy, the situation didn't lend itself to trust. Escorting the ex-hostages made them entirely too vulnerable to trust anyone who wasn't wearing Peacekeeper camos. Every so often the boy would pause and wait for something unseen before moving out again. Each time Ironstone focused his scope in on him, ready to zero him if it looked as if he was going to betray them.

Back with the lead elements of Stuart's Second Platoon, Rosemont followed Kat's progress through the taclink and was growing more impatient with every minute. Even with the kid guiding them, their progress through the city was dangerously slow. The longer it took for them to break free of the built-up area, the more time the Simbas had to discover that they had escaped and come looking for them.

Rosemont had discovered, just as Kat had, that their biggest problem was that the helmet nav displays were useless in this part of the city. Flying the Bat overhead had been a good idea, but the recon flyer wasn't picking up much information they could use. The clutter of small buildings and maze of back alleys and side streets gave confusing readings and rendered the recon data useless. It was ironic that the most sophisticated military technology in the world could be countered by primitive living conditions. But then the Bats had been designed to operate over battlefields, not over crowded slums.

Though Rosemont was anxious to be clear of the city, he resisted the urge to order Strider Alpha to move faster. The last thing they needed was to stumble into an ambush tonight. The only thing he could do was keep tightly behind her and make sure that everyone kept his finger on the trigger.

ROBERT HAD LED Kat and Ironstone a third of the way through the city when a small Simba patrol suddenly appeared from a darkened side alley. The recon grunts barely had time to slide back into cover, but Robert was caught out in the open. When he tried to run, the Simba patrol leader grabbed the boy's arm and slammed him up against the wall of a shack.

Holding on to Robert tightly, the Simba roared something at him in a language Ironstone didn't understand. The boy shook his head, and the Simba drew back his hand. The sound of the blow carried to the recon grunts, but they did nothing. There was nothing they could do for the kid without giving themselves away. Even though Ironstone couldn't understand what was being said, the Indian kept the boy in his sniper sights as the Simba continued to question him. At the slightest sign that the kid was giving away their presence, he'd zero him cold. By now the rest of the team had deployed around him and, if he had to shoot, they would take out the patrol.

After several more questions, the Simba patrol leader cuffed the boy on the side of the head one last time and sent him running on his way. Without even a glance in the Peacekeepers' direction, the Simbas moved off the other way down the alley.

Ironstone relaxed his trigger finger and brought his rifle down, but he and Kat kept under cover until the patrol was well out of sight. Now that the kid was gone, they were as good as lost again. She was about to key her mike implant and report to Rosemont when she heard a hiss from behind her. Spinning around, she saw Robert standing close to the wall.

"Missy," the boy said in heavily accented English. "I come back. I no leave you."

Kat resisted the urge to hug him. "Are you hurt?" she asked.

He shook his head.

Ironstone knelt at the boy's side and started questioning him in Afrikaans. The boy spoke softly but urgently in answer to Ironstone's questions.

"What's he saying?" Kat asked, anxious to get on the way again.

"He says that we have to be even more careful now," Ironstone translated. "The Simbas know that we left the stadium and they're hunting for us."

"Do you have any more good news, Ironman?"

The Indian grinned in the dark. "He also says that Madame Jumal has ordered them to kill all of us or to kill themselves in disgrace. The Simbas have vowed that if they take any of us alive, they're going skin us before slowly killing us."

"I don't need to hear that kind of dog shit, Ironman," Kat snapped. "No one lays their fucking hands on a Peacekeeper prisoner and lives to brag about it."

Ironstone didn't reply to his team leader's outburst. He had forgotten that she had been taken captive by the Islamic Brotherhood during their last operation. In the brief time she had been held prisoner, she had been raped. Later she had taken her bloody revenge for the outrage, but apparently that hadn't been enough. The incident had neither been forgotten nor forgiven.

"We'd better flash this back to the major," the sniper said, his eyes scanning the darkness. "And get our asses moving again."

"That's most affirm," Kat said as she keyed her mike implant.

HALF AN HOUR LATER Ironstone and Kat were still up on point as they continued to follow Robert through the maze of alleys and side streets. It was well past midnight and a full moon had risen, casting a dim, silvery light over the area. Even with their chameleon suits automatically adjusting to the patches of light and darkness, the two grunts kept to the deepest shadows.

The boy also kept tight to the sides of the shacks as he worked his way down the cluttered alley. The area they were passing through suddenly opened up into a cleared space on the left, containing a large walled enclosure surrounding what looked to be a two-story factory building. Kat automatically scanned the brick building as she went by, but she detected no signs of movement.

On the far side of the walled compound, the alley went back to being a rat's warren of shacks. Kat and Ironstone moved into cover behind the first of the huts and waited for the rest of the Strider Alpha body to catch up. The other three recon grunts had just joined up with them when, high in the air, a flare suddenly burst into life throwing a flickering yellowish light over the street in front of the factory compound. The second story of the factory erupted with fire from over a dozen windows, catching Stuart's lead squads out in the open.

"Take cover!"

As the grunts scrambled for cover in the shacks opposite the factory, a storm of automatic-weapons fire followed them. Once under cover, the Peacekeepers instantly returned fire, their red tracers crisscrossing with the green tracers from the Simba weapons.

While the grunts went into their counterambush techniques, trying to achieve fire superiority, Rosemont quickly took stock of their situation. Even though they were still in the city, this was one time when he sure as hell could have used the Bat's data input, but the recon flyer had gone off station for refueling. They were going to have to do this one on their own, trusting to their night imagers and sensors.

Just when it looked as if the grunts were getting the upper hand, a Simba antitank rocket launcher went into action. The first rocket hit a shack sheltering several grunts. The explosion shattered the flimsy structure and sent fragments of roofing tin and scrap lumber flying. The second round detonated against the corner of another shack, collapsing it on top of the Peacekeepers who had taken shelter inside.

Rosemont was keying his mike implant to order the grunts to pull back farther when Browning called over his borrowed comlink. "Major, Browning here," the hostage leader reported. "We're over by the gate at the left corner of the wall, and I've got the rocket launcher in sight. We're going in after it."

"Wait one," Rosemont said. "Let me send one of my squads in there."

"No, Major." Browning's voice was firm. "This time we are not going to run, we are going to fight."

There was nothing Rosemont could answer to that.

Shouting battle commands in Afrikaans, Browning led his group through the gate. Their captured weapons blazing, the ex-hostages charged the Simba position. Since they weren't wearing taclinks Rosemont could only follow them by the sounds of their weapons once they passed through the gate. A massive explosion in that direction was followed by a lull in the firing.

"Major, Browning here. You can go ahead, the launcher's been taken out."

"Good work."

"Our pleasure, Major."

Kat and her recon team found themselves on the far edge of the battle. While the recon grunts fired in support of the Second Platoon as they closed in on the compound wall, Ironstone unlimbered his scoped rifle and searched for targets in the factory's second-story windows. A muzzle-flash drew his attention, and he triggered two quick shots at it. The Simba rifleman made the mistake of firing again, and this time the Indian's return fire took him out.

Several rounds splattered against the sheet tin above the sniper, and he looked for the source of the fire. His IR sensors showed a heat trace at the corner of the building's flat roof farthest from him. Focusing his sniper scope on that area, he spotted the glowing green shape of a figure crouching behind the top of the wall and aiming a rifle down at the grunts rushing the compound wall. Ironstone's first shot took the Simba in the throat, snapping his head back. The insurance shot went into his back as he slumped over onto the roof.

By now two squads of Stuart's grunts had reached the safety of the compound wall and it was time to get serious. Storming a building was never easy, particularly when you had to cross a wide-open killing ground to reach it. Keying his mike implant, the platoon leader ordered everyone to put out maximum fire to cover the assault teams.

With their LARs switched down to full automatic fire, the Peacekeepers laced the front of the factory with fire. As soon as one of the 100-round plastic magazines ran empty, a fresh one was snapped in place and the withering barrage continued.

Under the cover of this deadly wall of 5 mm fire, Stuart's first assault team dashed up to the factory. Placing their entrance charge against the brick wall, they backed away and triggered the explosives. Before the smoke and dust even cleared, they rushed through the two-meter hole in the wall, their LARs blazing as they cleared the area inside. Once it was secured, they signaled for the second assault team to join them. Inside the factory the two teams went to work clearing the building room by room.

Outside, the grunts switched off their supporting fire and went back to searching out specific targets. Flashes appeared at the windows of the factory as the assault teams used EHE grenades to clean the rooms before they went in. A few bursts of fire later, a flash would appear at the next window.

Halfway through clearing the ground floor, the battle was over. The Simbas who had not been killed abandoned the building and took to their feet down the alleys. Another squad joined the assault teams and they fanned out in the building to carefully check it, room by room, for "stay-behinds." A few minutes later the all clear was sent.

The rest of Second Platoon came out of their positions and started policing up the battlefield. The hostile dead were left where they had fallen, and more than one wounded Simba was helped on his way to whatever he believed was awaiting them in the next world. This was no time to be concerned about treating hostile wounded.

Rosemont found Browning with his wounded. Unprotected by body armor, the ex-hostages had suffered serious casualties, including two killed. One of their dead was a teenage boy, the other a middle-aged man, and both had died assaulting the rocket launcher squad. Several more had been wounded, including one man with a serious chest wound who would probably not last the hour.

The platoon medics were patching up the last of the wounded and Browning was talking quietly with one of them when Rosemont walked up. The company commander glanced down at the two bodies lying against the base of the enclosure wall. "Do you want us to mark these two for later recovery?"

Browning shook his head. "No, Major, they're coming with us. If we leave them here," he explained, "the Simbas will mutilate them. We will carry them out ourselves so they can receive proper burial."

Rosemont nodded. The Peacekeepers never left their dead behind, so why should these people feel any different about their casualties? "As long as you can keep up with us," he said, "I don't see a problem."

"We will keep up, Major," Browning vowed. "Never fear about that."

"Okay, then," Rosemont said. "You'd better get 'em gathered up. We'll be moving out immediately." This little firefight would bring every Simba within a thousand meters running, and he wanted to get the hell out of the area before more trouble showed up.

ROBERT MOTOBU STOPPED in the shadow of a shack and motioned for Ironstone to come forward. When the Indian joined him, Kat saw the boy point to something in front of them and she focused her imager on the area. To her surprise, it looked clear and open.

"He says it's open bush beyond that next row of shacks," Ironstone reported. "And if we keep away from the roads, we should be okay."

Kat quickly relayed the information back to Rosemont, who ordered her to hold her team there until the main body joined up with them. While they waited, Kat thanked Robert and offered him payment for his assistance. As always, the Peacekeepers had been given a basic issue of the local currency to be used in an emergency, and she knew she would have no trouble getting this expenditure approved.

"No." Robert shook his head. "I no take money."

Kat pressed the wad of currency into his hand. "Take it for your family, buy food, buy books for school. I am sure you can find a use for this."

Reluctantly the boy pocketed the money. "Thank you, missy."

"Thank you, Robert, you saved our lives."

"Maybe I see you again some day, missy," the boy said shyly.

Kat reached out and took his hand. "I sure hope so, kid. Good luck."

With a final wave, the boy disappeared back into the maze of the Johannesburg slums.

11

In the Brush, August 13

Dawn was just breaking over the rolling South African veld when Rosemont's column came to a small stand of trees and the company commander called a halt. After they had broken out into the open, the refueled Bat had come back on station and had shown him a safe route to follow around the roving Simba patrols. Because of the Rapier missiles with the Simba forces, he hadn't called in the aircraft to pick them up and risk losing them.

Though they had been burdened with their dead and wounded, Rosemont had kept his grunts and the ex-hostages on the move throughout the rest of the night, stopping to rest only five minutes out of every hour. Now that the sun was coming up and they were within an hour's march of the airfield, he wanted to give everyone a long, well-deserved break before the final push to the airstrip.

Even his troops were starting to show their exhaustion, and several of them had already started taking the issue stimtabs. They had been operating now for over twenty-four hours without either rest or adequate rations, and it was beginning to tell on them.

Having been on short rations for the past several days, the ex-hostages were in even worse condition. But like the grunts, they didn't complain. Anything was better than what they had faced back at the stadium.

After setting out a security perimeter, the weary grunts settled down to a breakfast of coffee, if they had any, or stimtabs if they didn't. As they had done with their field rations at the stadium, the Peacekeepers shared their coffee and stimtabs with the ex-hostages.

The first thing Rosemont did was to check in with Sullivan back at the airstrip. "Bold Racer, Bold Lancer."

"Racer, go," Sullivan answered.

"What's your situation, Racer?"

"We're loading up the last of the hostages now and we're just waiting around for you, Lancer. We can come out and get you now if you'd like."

"That's a negative, Racer," Rosemont replied. "I need a Dust-Off flight for our dead and wounded, but I want to keep everything else back there with you. We don't know where those bastards might pop up, and I don't want to split our resources. If we're attacked, we can run for it and call for help. But if they hit the airfield, you have to hold it for us."

"Affirm, Lancer," Sullivan replied. "I'll get that Dust-Off out to you right away."

Rosemont checked his data pad for his casualty figures. "I have three body bags and another nine wounded, so that's going to be two Bubble Top loads."

"Affirm, Lancer. Racer, out."

Rosemont found a tree to lean back against and gratefully sat down to wait for the Dust-Off. Even though he was dead-ass tired and couldn't remember when he had last slept, he knew it would be useless to try to take a nap now. All it would do would be to make him even fuzzier. Taking a stimtab, though, would only make it that much more difficult for him to rest when they did reach the airstrip, so he would just tough it out. In a couple more hours at the most, he'd be back at the airstrip, loaded up and on his way back home to Fort Benning. And as far as he was concerned, it wouldn't be a minute too soon.

He had to admit, though, that the operation hadn't gone all that badly. Even considering the numerous Intelligence failures at USEF headquarters, Echo Company had been able to pull this thing off. But then he had expected nothing less of them. The thing that had impressed him the most about the recent Middle East operation was the extreme mobility and flexibility of the Peacekeeper units. Their high mobility was a function of their vehicles and equipment, but their flexibility was more mind set than mere technology. And their flexibility had been tested to the maximum on this mission. He knew of no other military unit that could have pulled this operation off in only twenty-four hours.

Twenty minutes later the voice of the Dust-Off pilot came over Rosemont's earphones. "Bold Lancer, Hook Talon Delta on final to your location."

"Affirm, Talon Delta. Your Lima Zulu is the wood line north of my position."

"Talon, affirm. I have it in sight."

While one of the Bubble Tops circled protectively overhead, the other ship flared out for a landing beside the small stand of trees. In seconds the wounded were loaded aboard and the chopper rose back up in the air. The second Bubble Top landed and it, too, was quickly loaded. This time, however, three of the passengers were in body bags. Browning's critically wounded man had died during the night march. As soon as the second chopper joined up with the first, they banked away to the east and climbed for altitude.

Rosemont watched the two choppers fly off before returning to his tree. Now that the dead and wounded had been evacuated, he should be able to make better time when they moved out again. He had just gotten comfortable again when Kat Wallenska's urgent voice broke in over his earphones. "Bold Lancer, Strider Alpha."

"Lancer, go ahead."

"Alpha. I'm afraid we've got us a problem here, Lancer. I'm picking up the rear elements of a large Simba force, and it looks like they're heading directly for Bold Racer's position at the airfield."

"Lancer, affirm." He quickly checked her position on his tac display and saw that she was covering his eastern sector. "How many of them are there?"

"There's a shit-load of 'em, Lancer. At least a battalion, if not more."

"Affirm, Alpha," he answered. "That definitely constitutes a problem. Wait where you are, I'm coming up." Though he could have linked to Kat's imagers and sensors to display on his tac screen what she was seeing, he had to check this one out for himself.

When Rosemont slid in beside Kat, he saw that the recon sergeant hadn't been exaggerating about the hostiles' strength one bit. He could detect at least a hundred well-camouflaged Simbas moving through the scrub brush across their planned march route to the airfield. It appeared that they were the rear guard of a much larger hostile force and they were definitely headed for the airstrip. Sullivan was going to be in for a rough time in a just a little while.

Rosemont keyed his mike implant to call his XO. "Bold Racer, Bold Lancer."

"Racer, go," Sullivan answered.

"Lancer. You've got a large hostile force approaching your position," Rosemont reported. "The lead elements are about half an hour away from you."

"We know all about them, Lancer," Sullivan replied, a note of weariness in his voice. "I was just about to give you a call about them myself. We just got a Bat airborne again, and it picked them up a few minutes ago. It looks like they're moving in on us from three different directions and they're coming on fast. We're digging deeper and I'm getting ready to evacuate the last of the transport aircraft now. Also I want to send the Bubble Tops with them. We've picked up multiple antiaircraft missile readings, and I don't want to risk sending the gunships up against them."

Losing the gunships would make it more difficult to defend the airstrip, but there was no point in sending them up simply to be shot down.

"Go ahead," Rosemont concurred. "Tell Talon Lead to get well out of range of the missiles, but to keep his turbines hot in case we have to use him."

"Racer, affirm," Sullivan replied. "That's what I told him. Also Force HQ has been apprised of our situation, and help's on the way. There's a platoon of the Bulls at the evacuation point, and they're in the air on their way to us now, ETA about an hour and a half. We should be able to hold 'em off till they get here."

"Lancer, affirm," Rosemont acknowledged the good news. "I'm going to try to move in a little closer and see if I can find a way to give you a hand."

"Racer, affirm."

ROSEMONT COULD HEAR the fighting around the airfield long before they had drawn within range. A half hour's march had put them close enough to hear the battle, but the point element was reporting large concentrations of Simbas directly between them and the airstrip. With the freed hostages accompanying him, there was no way he could throw his grunts against the Simba's rear and fight their way through to the airstrip. Too many of the ex-hostages had already been killed or wounded in this operation, and he didn't want to add to their casualties. His job had been to rescue them, not get them killed.

For better or for worse, Sullivan's First Platoon and the support troops at the airfield were on their own until the promised reinforcements could arrive. He couldn't resist the urge to see how the battle was going.

"Bold Racer," he called to Sullivan. "Bold Lancer, sitrep."

"This is Bold Racer. We're holding our own, Lancer," Sullivan reported. "But they're starting to bring out the heavy stuff. We're taking mortar fire right now, and they're using rocket launchers against our positions. Rivera's firing counterbattery fire, but they're zeroing in on him now and he just lost one of his tubes."

"Lancer. Tell him to get his people in their holes until the Bulls arrive. There's no sense in losing the whole platoon."

"That's affirm, they're going now."

"Lancer. We've come up against the trail elements and can't get any closer, so I don't think we'll be able to help. Since we're sitting along their avenue of retreat, I'm going to pull back to the east and get out of their way. When the Bulls show up, I don't want to get caught up in the rout."

"Affirm, Lancer," Sullivan answered. "One way or the other, we'll be here when you get back."

The sounds of the battle followed Rosemont as he turned and fled deeper into the bush. For the first time in his life as a professional soldier, he was running from the sound of the guns, rather than toward them, and it was a bitter thing.

AT THE AIRSTRIP, Mick Sullivan was up to his ass in alligators. Now he really knew how Colonel Travis had felt at the Alamo. His First Platoon and the airstrip support troops were well dug in, but there were far too few of them to win this one on their own. There were simply too damned many Simbas and they were well armed. For every one that his grunts put down, two more popped up in his place.

So far, the only reason that they hadn't been overrun already was that the Simbas were launching their attacks against his perimeter at only one place at a time. It was relatively easy for him to shift his forces to reinforce the sector being hit. But if the Simbas got their act together and hit him from two sides at once, it would get critical in very short order.

The northern sector of the perimeter suddenly erupted in fire. The Simbas hadn't tried that side yet, and it looked as if it was their turn in the barrel. Sullivan was flashing orders to reinforce that sector when a welcome voice broke in over his earphones. "Bold Racer, this is Dusty Lightning. We are overhead and are commencing the drop."

"Racer, affirm," he replied. "It's about time, Lightning, get 'em coming. They're all over our asses down here."

"You just stay frosty down there, Bold Racer," came the voice of Major Jim Collins, the Bravo Company CO. "The Bulls are here and the situation is well in hand."

That was easy for Collins to say; he wasn't facing a never-ending horde of howling Simbas. At least not yet. Sullivan would see how frosty Big Jim stayed once his ass was on the ground.

"Talk to me about the situation after you get down here, Lightning."

Collins laughed. "I'm launching now. See you in a minute, Mick."

Suddenly the skies over the beleaguered airfield were filled with the parachutes of the descending drop capsules of the Bravo Company Bulls. A ragged cheer went up from the grunts in their fighting holes when they saw the chutes. Now that help was at hand and they didn't need to conserve their ammunition, they increased their fire to cover the drop.

The greater volume of fire kept some Simba heads down, and while welcome, it wasn't really necessary. The big difference between the recon capsules that Echo Company had used to drop on the airfield and Bravo Company's heavy infantry capsules was that the Hulk drop capsules were armored against small-arms fire. The Hulks weren't helpless targets on their descent the way the recon grunts had been. They could fight effectively from their capsules if they needed to. And they needed to now as the Simbas opened up on them from all sides.

Sullivan saw one of the descending powered fighting suits light up as several streams of hostile tracer fire converged on it. The Hulk shook off the hostile fire and emerged unscathed, his weapons blazing. And, unlike the grunts, the Hulks were well armed for this kind of work. Their 8 mm M-18 Heavy Infantry Rifles, or HIRs, were more than just a bigger version of the fast-firing but light 5 mm LARs.

While the 8 mms fired somewhat slower than the lighter assault rifles, they made up for it with the greater power the larger projectiles delivered to the target. Also the Hulks' HIRs were fitted with a 30 mm grenade launcher under the barrel. The 30 mms fired the same EHE warheads as the Bubble Top launchers, but with a reduced propellant load. Even so, they could still reach out to seven hundred and fifty meters with pinpoint accuracy.

The authoritative bark of the 8 mms could be heard over the chatter of the lighter weapons as the Hulks rained fire down on the hostiles. The 30 mm EHE grenades arched down to take out the Simba automatic-weapons positions. Under the storm of fire from the descending Hulks, the Simba attack on the northern sector faltered and broke apart. Sullivan's taclink showed them pulling back into the bush.

"Dusty Lightning," Sullivan sent to Collins. "Racer. You'd better hurry up, they're getting away from you."

"Hold your water, Racer," Collins said. "We're touching down now."

The Hulks' capsules blew apart automatically as soon as their feet touched the ground, freeing them for instant combat. Once on the ground, they got to work doing what they did best—seriously kicking ass and taking names.

Joining up in pairs, they charged the hostile positions, totally ignoring the Simbas' return fire. The heavy infantry powered fighting suits were armored to withstand small-arms fire up to fifty caliber. Even the fifties needed to fire AP rounds to punch through their tough ceramal armored skins. The servos, gyros and boost units allowed a Hulk to run at twenty-five miles per hour while dodging enemy fire and firing his battery of weapons in return.

Against the unarmored Simbas, it was as if the Hulk suits were small tanks running with legs instead of tracks. And, like tanks, they easily broke through the Simba encirclement. Once they had punched a hole in the hostile line, they fanned out to either side and started clearing the perimeter.

One Simba, terrified by a man-shaped machine that he couldn't kill, tried to run from it. The powered suit easily caught up with him and stomped him into the dry earth. Other Simbas tried to stand and fight, but were unable to stand before the concentrated fire of the Hulks' HIRs. Like ripe grain before the threshing machine, the Simbas either ran or died in place.

In minutes the Hulks had completed their circle of the airstrip and had resecured the perimeter. Pausing only to reload, they fanned out into the brush to pursue the fleeing hostiles and to clear a wider security zone.

Now Sullivan's grunts left their holes and accompanied the Hulks on their rampage. Even though the powered suits were armored, they were still vulnerable to antitank weapons, and the light infantry grunts worked with them the way they would have with tanks, covering their flanks and screening for rocket launcher teams hiding in the brush.

Now that the Simbas and their antiaircraft missiles had been pushed away from the airfield, Sullivan could bring the Bubble Tops back into action. "Hook Talon, Bold Racer," he called to the gunships who had waited out the battle safely beyond the range of the missiles. "You can come home now. Dusty Lightning has the situation well under control."

Talon Lead had been sitting in his cockpit with his finger on the start trigger for his ship's turbine for the past hour and didn't need to be asked twice. "Hook Talon, that's most affirm," he sent back. "Tell the Bulls to leave a few of them for us, Racer."

"That's most affirm, Talon. But you'd better hurry up."

"Talon Flight cranking now."

12

In the Bush, August 13

From their new position in the bush half an hour's march east of the airfield, Rosemont followed the progress of the battle through a taclink to Bold Racer. Now the Bulls were on the ground, the Simbas were learning that it didn't pay to go head-to-head with power-suit heavy infantry. The way it was looking, the Hulks would have things cleaned up in short order and it wouldn't be a minute too soon for Echo Company, either. There were still some minor wounds to be tended to, his troops needed to be fed, and they were badly in need of an ammunition resupply, as well.

Rosemont was watching a Simba counterattack break apart under the concentrated fire from a pair of Hulks and a squad of Sullivan's grunts when Wallenska's voice broke in over his earphones. "Lancer, Strider Alpha. I'm afraid we have visitors again."

Rosemont sprang to his feet. As low on ammunition as they were, if a second Simba unit had discovered them, they were in deep shit. "Who are they?"

"I'll be damned if I know, Lancer. They look like something out of an old *National Geographic* special on African tribal life. They're armed with spears and shields, but they're holding their right hands out empty, so I think they're friendly."

"I'm coming up. Keep 'em under cover, but don't shoot unless you have to."

"Alpha, affirm."

He looked around, spotted Browning and motioned him over. "What do you know about the natives around here?"

"This is right on the edge of the Zulu country," he said. "And if you've spotted any natives, my bet is that they're Zulus."

"You don't happen to speak the Zulu language, do you?"

"No, I don't, Major." Browning shook his head. "But many of them speak either Afrikaans or English. Before the collapse of the old government, the Zulus put a great deal of effort into giving their people a decent Western education."

"Let's just hope that they've continued that particular tradition," Rosemont said. "I really need to talk to these people."

Now that the battle at the airstrip was winding down, the last thing Rosemont needed to discover was that he had another enemy to fight. All he wanted to do was deliver the remaining ex-hostages to the airstrip and then get Echo Company the hell out of this part of Africa.

When Rosemont reached Strider Alpha's position, he saw that Kat was right again—this did look like a scene out of a documentary holovee program on African tribal life in the previous century. The five men waiting for him wore little more than loin coverings, and bands of white hair were tied around their lower legs. They were armed with assegais, short stabbing spears, machetelike knives and oblong cowhide shields.

"They're Zulus, all right, Major," Browning said as another twenty warriors stepped out of the bush and stood silently behind the first group. "A big war party."

Only about a quarter of the Zulus were armed with firearms, and none of their guns was modern. The most common weapons were well-used Han Empire Type 98 5.56 mm assault rifles dating back to around the turn of the century. Though they were outdated, the Type 98s were efficient weapons and still a favorite in most of Africa and the Middle East. The rest of the warriors were carrying the same short spears and shields as their leaders.

Covered by the guns of Kat's team, Rosemont slung his LAR upside down over his right shoulder and stepped forward. "I am Major Alexander Rosemont of the American Peacekeeper Force. Do any of you speak English?"

A middle-aged warrior stepped forward. A stocky man of medium height, he held himself like a king as he strode up to Rosemont. Like the others, he was dressed in a loincloth, but he had tufts of white hair tied around his upper arms, as well as on his lower legs, and wore a leopard skin headband. The impression that he was a character from a historical holovee was broken only by the large gold Rolex watch he wore on his right wrist.

"I am John Ka Umkhonto," the Zulu said proudly, extending his right hand Western fashion. "Leader of the amaZulu. You and your American Peacekeepers are welcome to our land, Major Rosemont."

Rosemont shook his hand. "Thank you."

The Zulu looked at Browning, who was standing back with Kat Wallenska and her recon grunts and nodded to him. "We also welcome our white brothers who have escaped from Madame Jumal's clutches."

Back in the days of twentieth-century South Africa, the Zulus had often been allied with the whites and there had been a great mutual respect between the two peoples. In the final days of the white minority government, the Zulus had shared power with the whites, but there hadn't been enough of them to counter the influence of the more radical black factions when the new government was formed.

The radical politics of the Bantu People's Democracy had not only stripped all remnants of political power away from the whites who had remained behind, but it had also shut the Zulus out of the corridors of government. That wasn't their only punishment, though. In revenge for their having supported the whites in the old days, Madame Jumal had conducted pogroms against the Zulus, sending her Simbas into their unarmed villages to rape, kill and plunder.

Once a proud, powerful people in this part of Africa, the Zulus had been driven from their towns and villages and reduced to living in the bush with their cattle as their ancestors had done centuries before. That was why so many of them were dressed in traditional garb and were armed with shields and spears. What few firearms they possessed had been taken from dead Simbas. The proud Zulus might not be kings on their own land any longer, but they hadn't forgotten how to fight. Madame Jumal's Simbas entered Zulu territory at their peril.

"You and your people must be hungry," Ka Umkhonto said. "It is a long way from Johannesburg, and you have been on the march all night. We will feed you."

Rosemont didn't bother to ask how the Zulu knew that they had been on the move all night. From what he was learning about Africa, there was not much that went on without someone knowing about it.

"Thank you," Rosemont replied. "We could use something to eat."

Ka Umkhonto called out in Zulu and, as if materializing from out of nowhere, more warriors appeared with bags of maize meal and butchered quarters of fresh meat. Women with plastic jugs of water and cooking gear followed close behind them. Before long, several small fires were started, and the maize meal cakes that were a staple of the southern African diet were baking. Strips of meat also roasted over the flames, sending a savory aroma into the cool morning air. The ex-hostages gathered close to the cook fires, their mouths watering as they watched the women cook.

As soon as the maize cakes were done, the Zulus passed them to the whites, who wolfed them down without even waiting for them to cool off. Sizzling strips of broiled meat soon followed, and those, too, were devoured ravenously.

The Peacekeepers' mouths watered at the smell of the roasting meat, but they let the ex-hostages eat their fill first. The grunts were hardened to going with short rations. This wasn't the first time, nor would it be the last, that they had been hungry. Hunger they could deal with, but the lack of coffee was more serious for most of them. As with every Western army since the introduction of the coffee bean from the Middle East back in the sixteenth century, the Peacekeepers were fueled with caffeine.

"I'd kill for a cup of coffee right now," Rosemont growled as he watched the ex-hostages eat.

Stuart grinned. "Would instant coffee do?"

"You have coffee?"

"I always have coffee, sir. I've been taking lessons from the XO in how to make brownie points with the boss."

"Remind me to promote you to captain as soon as we get home."

"Promises, promises."

Rosemont laughed.

As soon as all the ex-hostages had eaten their fill, the Peacekeepers lined up for their breakfast, Zulu style. It wasn't quite USEF-issue field rations, but it would do nicely and the grunts had worked up a good appetite.

"You ready for a little mystery meat and corn cakes for breakfast?" Ironstone asked Kat Wallenska as they stood in the chow line.

"Right now I'm hungry enough to eat the ass end out of a skunk," she growled.

Ironstone grinned. "Sorry, Kat. Skunk's ass isn't on the menu, only roast whatever it is."

"Shit, if they can eat it, I can, too."

As soon as Rosemont and the grunts had eaten their fill, the Zulu leader approached him. "Now that you have shared our food," Ka Umkhonto said, "I would like to share our information with you, as well."

Rosemont frowned. "What do you mean?"

"There is an army invading my country, an army of whites. These are the whites who went away when the old government fell. Now they have come back and they are sweeping everything before them."

Rosemont was stunned. He could only be talking about the Boer exiles. What in the hell were they doing back in Africa? The last he knew, they were well established in their adopted country of Argentina. "Are you sure about this?"

The Zulu nodded gravely. "Several of my young men have been killed and even more have been wounded by them. When they crossed the border from Mozambique and entered our lands, we approached them in peace and they fired on us. We fought back, but they are well armed and difficult to kill."

Rosemont could well appreciate that. If the Boers were back, they were sure to be equipped with the best weapons money could buy, and modern firearms made anyone hard to kill when all you had to do it with were spears and shields.

"I will be rejoining the rest of my Peacekeeper unit at the Malaika airstrip soon," Rosemont said. "I would like you and your people to come with us and talk to my commander back in the United States. Maybe we can do something to stop these people."

Ka Umkhonto nodded. "We will come with you. This is a great danger to all of us here, not just to the

Zulus. I fear that these whites have come to take the land away from us again."

Knowing what he did of the Boer exiles, Rosemont thought that the Zulu's fears were well justified. Even though they were no longer headline news, stories regularly appeared about the Boers' holdings in Argentina and their dreams of returning to their old homeland. If they were back, he could bet that they intended to stay.

BACK AT THE AIRSTRIP, Sullivan's grunts and the Bravo Company Hulks were just mopping up the last few diehard Simbas when Rosemont's grunts appeared. The Peacekeepers had been warned that the Zulus were accompanying Rosemont, but they were still surprised when they saw the African warriors come out of the bush. Weapons were instantly trained on them and Rosemont quickly flashed a stand-down signal over the comlink.

The airstrip and the surrounding area were littered with bodies and the debris of battle. Simba bodies lay where they had fallen, but the Peacekeepers were busily policing up their fallen arms and ammunition. When Rosemont saw Ka Umkhonto's Zulus eyeing the weapons, he made a mental note to ask Force HQ if he could release them to the Zulus.

Unless they had orders to destroy a government, the Peacekeepers tried not to upset the balance of power in the nations they operated in. But considering the circumstances here, he was sure that Force HQ would make an exception in this case. Even though they did not have orders to put Madame Jumal's government out of business, all of southern Africa would sleep easier if she and her Simbas were history and a moderate leader was installed in the so-called Bantu People's Democracy. Maybe even a moderate Zulu leader with Western leanings.

Before he got involved with that, however, he had to see that the last of Madame Jumal's current crop of victims got sent on their way to safety. The hostage evacuation team quickly gathered up Browning and his men and ran them through the medical aid station set up in the burned-out hangar. As soon as all their wounds and injuries were tended to, they were offered food and drink and a place to rest until the evacuation planes could return safely.

Once Major Collins flashed the message that the area surrounding the airstrip was completely cleared of hostiles, Rosemont had Sullivan call for the Tilt Wing transport to come back in to pick up Browning and the last of his people.

As soon as he received word that the plane was on its final approach to the airstrip, Rosemont sought out the leader of the ex-hostages. Browning was drinking from a Peacekeeper readi-heat coffee canister when he walked up. "Your plane will be landing shortly," the company commander said. "And you'll be joining the others in just a few hours."

Browning held out his hand. "Thanks ever so much, Major Rosemont. We all owe both you and your people a great debt."

"I'm sorry we had to meet this way," Rosemont said, shaking his hand.

Browning's eyes flicked over to the three body bags awaiting transport. "So am I, Major. But it would have been far worse if you hadn't rescued us. We will never be able to thank you enough."

"No thanks are needed," Rosemont said modestly. "This is what we do for a living."

Browning smiled thinly. "It is a tough way to make a living."

"It has its moments," Rosemont agreed, "but it has its rewards, as well. And this is one of those times."

"Thank you again and good luck."

"You take care."

As soon as the transport landed, the pilot dropped his rear ramp and prepared for immediate boarding. Even though the Simbas had faded back into the bush, he wanted to load and be on his way as soon as possible. It was only a matter of minutes for the ex-hostages to be boarded and strapped down for the flight. As soon as the crew chief raised the rear ramp, the Tilt Wing pilot ran his twin turbines back up to speed. With its two big rotors beating the air, the ship rose in a flurry of dust.

As soon as the Tilt Wing transitioned to level flight and disappeared to the north, Rosemont flashed a message to the Bravo Company commander, Jim Collins, to meet him at the communications center in the burned-out hangar. It was time that the two of them got on the horn back to Benning and got this Boer situation sorted out.

Malaika Airstrip, August 14

"I don't believe what I'm hearing," Ashley Wells exploded. "First these bastard Simbas do their best to wipe us off the face of the earth, and now we have to defend them? What in the fuck is the colonel thinking of? I lost some good people here and now I'm just supposed to kiss and make up? To hell with that shit!"

Rosemont sighed and took a deep breath. He had expected this response from Ash-and-Trash Wells. Subtlety wasn't her forte, and she didn't take well to the political nuances of war. To her, combat was purely a black-and-white affair. Once you had been designated an enemy, you were an enemy forever more. The only truce Ashley accepted was one when she had her boot on the back of a foe's neck grinding his dead face into the dirt.

The Zulu's report of an exile Boer invasion had been taken seriously by the USEF Headquarters back at Fort Benning. The first thing that was done to confirm the Zulu claim was to turn the deep-space recon satellites loose on southern Africa. When the satellite data was checked and the Boer column was discovered, confirmation was flashed to the jump CP at the airstrip and the Peacekeepers were put on alert to guard against the new threat.

An uneasy truce was quickly negotiated with Madame Jewel Jumal and her Simbas. The black leader hated all whites, Peacekeeper and Boer alike, with a passion that completely overwhelmed her. But even she realized that it would be to her advantage to have the Americans on her side to counter this new threat. Neither Jumal nor the Peacekeepers particularly liked this arrangement, but it was necessary for the moment. When the Boers had been dealt with, the truce would be reevaluated by both sides.

Rosemont didn't particularly care for his new allies, either, but orders were orders and he couldn't afford to get into a pissing contest with Ashley about them. "The situation has changed, Wells," he said patiently. "As you know, our original sanction was to come in and get the white hostages out, which, as you also know, we have done. Now, however, the situation has changed, and there is the matter of an invading army attacking this country. And as you also well know, invading your neighbor is a big no-no with the Peacekeepers. Therefore, our mission orders have been changed."

"But it's an army of Boer exiles, Major," she protested. "Since they're exiles, it makes it a civil war, and if I remember correctly, our charter specifically states that we don't get involved in civil wars."

"Ours not to reason why," Sullivan started quoting. "Ours but to do or..."

"Shut the fuck up, Mick," Ashley growled. "This is serious."

"You're right, Wells," Rosemont cut in abruptly. He wasn't up to listening to Ashley and Mick go at each other again. "It is serious, damned serious, and that's why the colonel's ordered us on alert until we can get this shit sorted out."

"Has anyone bothered to notify the Simbas that we're on their side?" Ashley pressed her point. "Do they know that we're supposed to be their friends now?"

"I'm sure that Pretoria has been properly notified," Rosemont said dryly.

"But what if they don't get the word to all their troops in the field? What do we do if we're fired on by our new 'friends'?"

Rosemont grinned. "If we're shot at, we will shoot back, but in a friendly manner."

"That sucks, Major."

Once again Rosemont had had about all he could take from his volatile, abrasive recon platoon leader. He'd thought that after the problems they'd had during the Middle East operation, she would have learned that there was a limit to just how much he would put up with from her. Goddammit! She could be an outstanding officer when she wanted to, so why couldn't she just shut the fuck up and soldier?

"I'll tell you what, Lieutenant," Rosemont said, his voice cold now. "Why don't you just trot your young ass on over to the CP, get on the horn and tell the colonel that you don't like the mission he's given us? I'm sure he'll want the benefit of your advice. I'm also sure he'll be glad to find a seat for you on one of the evacuation planes back to Benning right after he accepts your resignation."

There was a tense silence for a long moment. Service in the Peacekeepers was totally voluntary and not everyone could accept the rigid discipline of the elite organization. Anyone of any rank could resign, no questions asked, at any time when he wasn't actually under hostile fire. It was rarely done, but the provision was in the regulations nonetheless.

Rosemont broke the silence. "Are you still with us, Lieutenant Wells?"

"Yes, sir," Ashley bit out.

Rosemont locked eyes with her. "Good! Now that this matter has been settled to your satisfaction, may I get back to the briefing?"

Ashley nodded stiffly.

"The Zulus ran into the vanguard of this Boer army two days ago and they've been tracking them since then. They've had a couple of skirmishes with them, but haven't gotten heavily engaged. Nonetheless, they have taken casualties. Our mission is to make contact with these people and determine their intentions. We are also to direct them to turn around and leave the territory of the Bantu People's Democracy. Should, however, they refuse to turn around and go back the way they came, we are to back off and screen them until the Hulks can get in and deal with them. We are not to get heavily engaged unless we absolutely have to."

Ashley knew that she was now treading a fine line, but she couldn't help herself. "In other words, we're to put our asses on the line again and if they tear us up, the Hulks will come in and stomp them flat for us."

Rosemont took a deep breath. "In words of more than two syllables, Lieutenant, you are absolutely correct. We are going to put it on the line again in the name of preserving the peace. That's what we get paid for."

Ashley snorted. "I'd better check with the adjutant to make sure that my will is up-to-date."

"If I were you, I'd also check in with the transportation officer while you're at it. I've got a feeling that you're going to be needing his services before this operation is over."

"I said I was in, Major." She leaned forward, her voice intent. "And I meant every word of it. That doesn't mean, however, that I have to automatically agree with everything that goes along with it."

She raised her hand to forestall his reply. "But when Echo Company goes up against these assholes, I can assure you that recon will be up front, where they belong, and I'll be right up there with them."

"That's all I ask," Rosemont replied. There was nothing more that he could ask of any of his people.

WHILE THE PEACEKEEPERS awaited final clearance for the new mission, the Bat UAVs flew aerial recon missions against the Boer column. The recon flyers gave Rosemont a great deal of information about the hostile force he would be facing: its size, their weapons and their formations. It was all good battlefield Intelligence, but it didn't answer the biggest question he had about them. The Bats couldn't tell him the Boer's intentions.

They weren't driving straight on to Pretoria as he would have expected of an invading army that had the element of surprise on its side. Instead, they had given up the advantage of the momentum of the attack and were moving slowly, clearing the areas they passed through of all armed resistance. Obviously they were making sure that they left no one behind to cause them trouble later. These were the actions of an overly confident commander, someone who had no fear that he could possibly lose, and Rosemont didn't understand the Boer's confidence.

No matter how good you were, there was always the chance that the gods of war would roll the dice in favor of the other guy. This was basic to all military operations and had been the single constant truth throughout recorded human history. Battle was never a sure thing—absolutely never. Only a mad man, a Hitler or a Saddam, went to war without considering the possibility that he could lose, only a madman or a man who knew something that no one else knew.

It wasn't that the Simbas could be taken lightly as opponents; that much he knew. They were well armed, there were thousands of them, and once they responded to the Boer invasion, they wouldn't be overcome easily. Echo Company was lucky to have gotten off with as few casualties as they had in their contacts with them. They'd had the element of surprise working for them, but they'd still had to move fast to capitalize on it.

That advantage, however, was now lost for the Boers. The big question was, what did their commander know that had made him so confident that he had given up the advantage of striking swiftly at the heart of the enemy? What did he know, or perhaps even more important, what force did he have at his command, that would let him take his time this way?

This was what Rosemont desperately needed to know, and all he had to work with to find an answer was the data from the UAV flyers. When Force Headquarters released them to go back to work, he would send his recon teams in to gather some bare eyeball input. But for now the only thing he could do was go over the sensor readouts with the operations staff again and look for anything they might have missed the first time around.

While their commander searched for answers to his tactical questions, the men and women of Echo Company prepared for the mission to come. For most of them the stand down was a welcome respite and a chance to get their personal houses in order before they launched themselves into battle again.

The original hostage-rescue mission had been put together on such short notice that they weren't prepared for an extended operation. Now, however, they could go over their weapons, ammunition and equipment and make sure that every last item was as it should be. As professional soldiers, every Peacekeeper knew that his survival on the battlefield all too often depended upon a minor detail. Every one of them knew how often "for the want of a nail" a battle, or a life, was lost.

As soon as her weapons had been cleaned, her magazines reloaded and her grenades replenished, Kat Wallenska put them aside and started going over the rest of her gear item by item. As the leader of Echo Company's premier recon team, she knew that she would be up on point with her team when the company moved out again. But that was okay with her. In fact, Kat hated being anywhere but out on point.

When her comlink, sensors and tac display checked out in the green, she went over her assault harness and armored inserts. To her surprise, she found a nick on one of the ceramal thigh plates, but it didn't look bad enough to need replacing. Assembling and donning her gear again, she walked over to the supply point and drew three days' recon rations with extra readi-heat coffee canisters.

While she was there, she also drew extra salt tablets from the medics and borrowed another two-quart canteen from one of the support troops. In the brief time she had been in Africa, she hadn't yet acclimatized to the heat. Since she expected to be moving fast tomorrow, she didn't want to become a heat casualty.

Back at her Team's positions, she stowed her rations and sat back down in her fighting hole. Reaching down to her boot top, she drew her Teflon fighting knife and started honing the blade against the leather she had sewn to the inside of her left pant's leg. The blade had acquired a couple of nicks in it, and she hated a rough blade.

On the other side of the airstrip perimeter, Mick Sullivan finished his mission prep early and looked around for something to do. Even in the Peacekeepers, war was mostly waiting around for something to happen, and he was easily bored. Usually he had a small holovee player tucked away in his personal effects along with a good stock of holo disks of his favorite old movies. But he hadn't expected to be on the ground for more than twenty-four hours this time, and he had left the holovee player behind. Since he had nothing to watch to pass the time, maybe he could find someone to talk to.

Slinging his LAR over his shoulder, he wandered over to the Second Platoon sector, looking for Jeb Stuart. He found the Southerner kicked back, with his head on his ammo pouches, apparently asleep. Jeb opened one eye at Sullivan's approach. "You forgot your holovee player, didn't you?"

Sullivan pulled up a loose sandbag and, looking around the airstrip, sat down. "I hope Force turns us loose pretty quick. This isn't exactly the funnest place we've ever been."

"It beats the shit outta that Saudi desert we were in last time. At least there's trees to look at here." He glanced up at the sun. "And it's not half as hot. You ought to be glad we got sent here. They could have sent us to the Himalayas to referee that pissing contest between the Hans and the Nepalese."

Sullivan shuddered. If there was anything he hated worse than being bored, it was being cold and bored. "Bite your tongue, Jeb. I don't even want to hear about that place."

"You'd better buy yourself some long johns when we get back," Stuart replied. "Rumor has it that they were talking about sending us in right before this thing came up."

Sullivan looked pained. "I should have listened to my mother. She wanted me to be a lawyer."

Stuart laughed.

But Sullivan wasn't the only one having second thoughts. After thoroughly checking over her weapons and equipment, Ashley Wells wrote a brief letter to her registered next of kin, the legal firm of Butler, Butler and Associates in Los Angeles. In the letter she changed the terms of her will to include a large payment that was to be made to the Peacekeeper officers' club in the event of her death. With the money, which was to be used for a party in her memory, was to go a large gold-plated plaque that was to bear a very specific legend.

'I told you so, you stupid bastards'
First Lieutenant Ashley "Ash-and-Trash" Wells
2002-2030 A.D.

She smiled as she sealed the letter and took it over to the message center. She would play their stupid games like a good little soldier, but she would also have the last word. No woman could ever ask for more.

14

Malaika Airstrip, August 15

It was early the next morning when the Peacekeepers received their clearance for the mission. During the night Ka Umkhonto's Zulus had volunteered to guide Echo Company to the Boer column, and Rosemont had immediately accepted their offer. Clearing this arrangement through Force Headquarters back at Benning had taken a little longer, but Rosemont had insisted. Even with the nav aids and the UAVs, it never hurt to have an experienced local guide when you were moving through unfamiliar hostile territory.

Right at first light Rosemont sounded "Assembly" over the comlink, and Echo Company fell in at the edge of the airstrip to await their transport out to the bush.

"This looks like one of those living-history theme parks," Stuart said as he eyed the contingent of Zulu warriors in their traditional dress who were waiting with them. "Spears in the twenty-first century?"

"Did you ever see the classic Zulu war movies," Sullivan asked, "*Zulu* and *Zulu Dawn*?"

Stuart shook his head.

"You missed some real good flicks. These are the same guys who took on England's finest in the late 1800s and beat them flat into the ground. The only reason that the Brits won in the end was that they had unlimited firepower, artillery and horses. These guys may be carrying assegais and shields today, but they're some of the finest low-tech troops in the world."

"I'll take your word for it, but we aren't going to be hunting redcoats with muzzle loaders this time. We're going up against guys armed with modern assault rifles, and I'm just not all too sure that spears are going to be much good against them."

"You might be surprised," Sullivan said. "I'll bet these guys are pretty good at springing ambushes."

"They'd sure as hell better be," Stuart muttered, "or they're all going to wind up hyena meat."

Just then the two Tilt Wing assault transports spooled up their turbines and their rotors started spinning. The mount-up call on the comlink sent the grunts running for the birds. They were followed closely by their Zulu guides, who scrambled up the ramps after them.

This was the first time that most of the Zulus had ever flown in an aircraft and, while many of them were as excited about flying as children, some of them were clearly apprehensive about it. They grinned broadly to hide their fears as the grunts helped them stow their spears and shields and showed them how to belt themselves into the seats.

The crew chief sent a lift-off signal to the pilot, and he spooled up his turbines. Rising in a flurry of dust, the Tilt Wings lifted off, transitioned the wings to level flight and banked away to the east. Four armed Bubble Tops of Talon Flight quickly joined up with them, and Echo Company was on its way to war again.

SINCE THE BATS had detected large numbers of the French-manufactured Rapier antiaircraft missiles among the Boers' weaponry, the Tilt Wings landed at a cold LZ several klicks in front of the Boer lead elements. While the armed Bubble Tops circled protectively overhead, the Echo Company grunts quickly deplaned, formed up and moved out into the bush.

Sullivan's First Platoon took the point with two of the recon teams and the Zulu guides scouting his flanks for him. Five hundred meters back with Stuart's Second Platoon, Rosemont monitored the input from his lead elements on his tac display. Mick's people were moving slowly and cautiously, but the company commander didn't mind. In fact, he insisted on it.

In a reconnaissance in an operation like this, the last thing he needed to do was to force a contact that would result in a battle. As far as he was concerned, he had all the time in the world to scout these guys out and try to discover what they were doing before he bumped heads with them. At least this time, though, he had some extra firepower on call if things got tight.

Even though the Bubble Top gunships had flown off with the transports after dropping the grunts off, the Tilt Wings had flown on to another LZ, where they had landed again. There Hank Rivera's gunners had unloaded one of their 120 mm rocket mortars and set up a temporary firebase within range of the Peacekeeper column. If the contact went bad, they could provide covering fire while the grunts withdrew.

Rosemont switched to his fire-support frequency and keyed his mike implant. "Bold Thunder, Bold Lancer."

"Thunder Xray, go," the weapons platoon FDC answered.

"Lancer, sitrep."

"We're in place, Lancer, and monitoring the recon team tac input. The rounds are in the ready racks, and as soon as you need them, they'll be on the way."

"Lancer, affirm."

"LANCER, BOLD RACER." Sullivan flashed back to Rosemont with the Second Platoon. "We've got company—there's a dozen gunships coming in low from the northwest. From the looks of them, they're Simba Mangustas."

"Are they heading our way?"

"Negative, Lancer. It looks like they're going straight for the Boers."

"Affirm," Rosemont replied. "Keep 'em under observation. I still don't trust those bastards."

"That's most affirm, Lancer."

Sullivan watched the Simba gunships fly straight and level in a tight formation as if they were on a training mission. If these pilots had flown combat missions before, it could only have been against opponents who didn't have ground-to-air missiles in their arsenals. If these guys didn't go tactical in a big hurry, the Boers were going to tear them new assholes.

Suddenly dark streaks trailing fire and white smoke rose from the bush on the horizon. The Simbas finally broke their close formation, but it did them no good. The gunships were swatted from the air like so many bothersome flies. More Rapier missiles rose on trails of flame as their vectoring nozzles directed them straight into their targets.

Once the missile's homing warheads were locked on, there was little the Simba pilots could do to evade the deadly missiles. Two of the gunships collided in midair as they vainly tried to get out of the way. The Rapier they had tried to get away from hit their combined wreckage and detonated anyway.

The Simba air attack was over in seconds, and only one of the Mangusta gunships had escaped destruction. The bright blue African sky was stained with greasy black smoke from the burning wreckage.

"So much for tactical air support," Sullivan said dryly as he watched the death of the Simba gunships through his image enhancer.

At his side Kat Wallenska also watched the carnage. "We need to get some Scorpions in here," she said, referring to the hot new ground-attack fighter just now coming into service with the regular American forces. The Scorpions were fitted with the latest in ECM defenses against missiles and were said to be able to survive in any battlefield environment.

Sullivan finally turned his eyes away. "That's affirm. Helicopter gunships sure as hell aren't cutting it here today."

"Which means that we're back to basics."

"That's affirm." Sullivan snapped his visor down and shifted his LAR around on its sling so the pistol grip readily fell to hand. "When all else fails, send in the fucking infantry."

Kat smiled. "That's life in the Force, LT."

"That's most affirm."

ON THE LEFT FLANK of First Platoon, John Ironstone was teamed up with a young Afrikaans-speaking Zulu warrior. Armed with only a spear and shield, the Zulu moved quickly and silently through the bush like a stalking lion. Even with his Peacekeeper training and the experience he had gained on battlefields all over the world, the Indian was hard-pressed to keep up with him.

To Ironstone's right, Kat Wallenska was also working with one of the Zulu warriors, an older man with tribal scars on his cheeks. When they had been teamed up by the Zulu captain, the warrior had obviously not been pleased to learn that his American partner was to be a woman.

Coming from a warrior tradition himself, Ironstone had instantly noticed the man's reluctance. Using his hypno-induced Afrikaans, he quickly put the warrior straight on Kat's status. Pointing out the silver skull in her ear and the fighting knife on her boot sheath, he launched into a long recitation about her prowess as a woman warrior.

When the Indian had first joined recon, he had also had reservations about working with a woman and knew exactly what to tell the Zulu to calm his fears. When he was finished, the Zulu looked at her with new respect. Snapping his spear up in almost a salute, he put his shield in front of his face and started backing away from her.

"What in the hell did you say to that guy, Ironman?" Kat asked as the Zulu backed away from her.

"Not much." Ironstone shrugged. "I just told him that you drink your enemy's blood from their skulls and kill at least one man every day before breakfast."

"Why in the hell did you tell him that?"

Ironstone smiled broadly. "Just because you're a woman, I didn't want him to think that you're some kind of RA malf."

Kat's Zulu partner had only rudimentary English, but she was able to follow his hand signals as he wove his way through the bush. So far, beyond a few day-old animal trails, neither the recon grunts nor the Zulu scouts had spotted anything of interest. Apparently the Boers were keeping close to their main body.

Ashley was out on First Platoon's far right flank with the Strider Bravo recon team. Just like Kat Wallenska's Strider Alpha, she hadn't seen anything so far, either. The Bats were back at the airstrip for refueling right now, but their last data downlink had shown that the Boers were still several klicks away, moving at an angle across their axis of advance toward Jo'burg. At the cautious speed the Peacekeepers were moving, it would be at least another hour before they made contact with the Boer main body.

Ashley really didn't know what to expect when they finally did make contact with them. Her style of logic told her that since they were the enemies of her Simba enemies, they would be her friends. But she also knew the fallacy of that particular line of reasoning. Just because the Boers had been kicking the shit out of the Simbas didn't mean that they would welcome the Peacekeepers and the message they carried, particularly when that message was for them to turn around and go back the way they had come or pay the price.

She intended to treat the exiles with a great deal of caution until they had proven their good intentions by grounding their arms and turning their asses around.

Till then she wouldn't trust them any more than she trusted those bastard Simbas.

EVEN WITH THE ZULUS and the recon teams scouting for them, Sullivan's First Platoon walked straight into an ambush. The two recon teams were weaving back and forth across his front to cover a greater area and they were out on the far flanks when his lead element tripped the ambush. From a small rise in the ground, a dozen assault rifles opened up on them all at once.

First Platoon went to ground and immediately returned fire. Breaking an ambush depended upon sheer firepower, and the grunts all had their LARs switched down to full-auto as they went into the counterambush drill. A storm of 5 mm fire laced the bush and the small hill held by the hostiles. Small puffs of black smoke and a cloud of red dirt marked the spots where their 30 mm grenades hit.

Once fire superiority had been regained, the grunts went into the maneuver phase of their counterambush drill. Sullivan was well out in front of First Squad, leading the counterattack, when he heard more than felt the blow that slammed against the side of his helmet. His legs buckled, and the last thing that flashed through his mind was that he had forgotten to pay his mess bill this month and Rosemont was going to be pissed.

ROSEMONT WAS in the middle of issuing his fire command to Rivera's gunners when he hard a loud, warbling siren tone over his earphones, the emergency recall signal. This signal to disengage and pull back immediately was never sounded except in the most extreme emergencies, and it couldn't be ignored. This was the one order that had to be obeyed even if it cost lives. He immediately punched in the acknowledgment code and retransmitted the signal to the grunts.

Each of the Peacekeepers heard the warbling emergency recall tone over their comlinks at the same time. The grunts immediately halted in place, ceased firing, took cover and sent their acknowledgment.

Ashley heard the signal but didn't flash an immediate acknowledgment. She had seen Mick go down, and her tac display showed Mick's locator beacon two hundred meters away. His bio readout indicated that he was still alive, but she knew that could change in an instant. Signaling for Strider Bravo to follow her, she raced through the bush toward him.

"Bold Strider," Rosemont's voice sounded loud in her earphones. "This is Bold Lancer. Mike Six Charlie Xray Tango. Execute withdrawal immediately. Acknowledge."

Since Rosemont had given his orders in clear language instead of tac code and had transmitted the mission authentication and destruct code, she had no choice but to acknowledge instantly. Were she to do anything else, in sixty seconds he would assume she had been captured and would trigger the destruct capsule in her comlink, which would kill all of her tactical electronics and leave her blind.

"Lancer, Bold Strider. Lima Nine Charlie Xray Bravo. Acknowledge withdrawal. Executing now."

Ashley shot one last glance in the direction where Mick had gone down as she recorded the location in her imager data storage. Mick Sullivan could be a royal pain in the ass sometimes with his endless rambling on and on about old flatvee movies, but he was still a brother grunt and she'd be back to get him.

Dead or alive, the Peacekeepers didn't leave their own on the field of battle.

15

With the Boers, August 15

Mick Sullivan woke to find himself staring at the muzzles of a dozen assault rifles in the hands of white men dressed in veld camouflage uniforms of brown, tan and green. When he looked closer, he saw that the weapons were copies of the LARs his own troops were armed with, but these sure as hell weren't Peacekeepers—they were Boers.

One of the Boers barked a command in a Germanic-sounding language as he motioned with the muzzle of his LAR.

"Sorry, old chap," Sullivan said calmly as he sat up. "I'm afraid that I don't speak Afrikaans. English perhaps?" He didn't do his Alec Guinness imitation very often. But this situation seemed to call for staying frosty, and old Alec was very good at that. Hadn't he beaten his Japanese captors in *The Bridge on the River Kwai* by keeping a cool head?

"Can you stand?" the Boer asked him in strangely accented English.

"I think so." Sullivan slowly got to his feet, being careful not to make any sudden moves. His head was spinning and his ears rang. He didn't think he was seriously hurt, though, at least not yet. He stood stock-still while hands stripped him of his helmet, comlink and field gear and patted him down for hidden weapons. Unfortunately they found the hideaway knife he kept tucked away in the back of his belt. Worse still, they located and removed the sending unit for his personal locater beacon. Now he was completely on his own.

As soon as he was clean, the English-speaking Boer addressed him again. "If you give me your word that you will not try to run, I will leave your hands free."

The voice was polite, but the muzzles of the LARs didn't waver an inch and Sullivan had no doubt that if he tried to run they would shoot him down. The man was young and fit and had the look of an experienced field trooper, as did the rest of his men. Sullivan knew that the Boers often hired out as mercenaries, and these lads had apparently done enough time in the woods to know what they were doing.

"You have my *parole,* old chap."

"Come with us."

"Where are you taking me?"

"No talking, please."

Not wanting to push his luck, Sullivan shut up. He did notice, however, that the Boers moved through the scrub brush as professionally as did his own grunts. More often than not, mercenary training was haphazard, but mercenary trained or not, someone had taken the time to make real soldiers out of these exiles. No wonder they had been able to spring that ambush on his people. He had no doubt that Echo Company would teach these guys better manners the next time they met, but for now he had to admit that he was in deep shit.

After half an hour on the march, the small Boer patrol arrived at a densely wooded thicket along a riverbank. Backed in under the trees were a dozen or so armored skimmers, former Israeli army vehicles by the look of them, and two dozen more six-and-a-half-ton overland trucks of the variety that did commercial long-haul work all over southern Africa. The trucks had been repainted in matt finish camo over their colorful civilian livery.

Sullivan was taken to one of the skimmers, the command vehicle from the looks of the antennae sticking above the armor. Several figures in camouflage field uniforms were seated around the skimmer working at computer monitors and hard-copy maps. Obviously this was the command group.

He didn't have to be told who was in charge here. The tall man in his sixties with faded blue eyes, the white hair and full beard of a biblical prophet, dressed in a tan bush jacket, had to be the man.

"You are an American," the old Boer said as Sullivan was led up to him. He said it as a statement, not a question. "One of the Peacekeepers."

"Yes, sir, I am. Lieutenant Thomas Sullivan, Echo Company, United States Expeditionary Force."

The Boer studied him for a long moment, taking in his chameleon camos and the empty connectors where his comlink had been. "I am Jan Rikermann."

Sullivan noticed that the man did not identify the name of his organization, as if he expected Mick to know who he was. Maybe someone back at Force

Headquarters did, but he had sure as hell never heard of him.

"What is your force doing in South Africa?"

"We were ordered to the Bantu People's Democracy on a rescue operation," Sullivan stated, careful not to use the old Boer name for the country. "Hostages were being held by a military junta, and our mission was to free them. Our mission was successful."

"Madame Jewel Jumal and her Simbas hold the whole nation of South Africa captive," Rikermann's voice rang out. "Not just some of its white citizens."

"I don't know anything about that, sir. My orders were to free the hostages, nothing more."

"You were not freeing the hostages when your platoon engaged my troops."

"We were fired upon," Sullivan corrected him. "And it is SOP in the Peacekeepers that we always fire back when we are fired upon."

"SOP?"

"Standard Operating Procedures," Sullivan explained.

"But you have no sanction here," Rikermann said. "No reason to oppose us. This is not Johannesburg—we are not holding anyone hostage here."

Sullivan stood a little straighter and took a deep breath. Here it comes, he thought, but I can't let him get away with that one. "The United States Expeditionary Force does not need a sanction to defend itself," he said proudly. "No one fires on the Peacekeepers and gets away with it." He paused. "No one!"

Rikermann studied him for a long moment, a strange look in his faded blue eyes. Then he barked out a command in Afrikaans, and Sullivan felt hands on his arms again. As he was led away, he spotted another man in civilian clothes standing apart from the others in uniform. This man was dark haired, short and wiry, and looked completely out of place among the bigger, blond Boers. He would have looked more at home in the Middle East, and Sullivan wondered who he was.

THE BOER GUARDS escorted Sullivan to one of the skimmers hidden under the trees and handed him over to a four-man security detachment. The sergeant in charge patted him down for weapons again before pointing to a seat inside the open rear ramp door of the skimmer. Sullivan sat down and took careful stock of his surroundings. Without his helmet and com gear, he had only the vaguest idea of where he was. If he got a chance to evaporate, he needed to know which way to start running.

Under the thick canopy of the trees he couldn't see the sun. He didn't know the time anyway without his comlink, so he couldn't navigate that way. Peering into the dim interior of the fighting vehicle, he spotted the instrument panel in front of the driver's position. In the upper right-hand corner of the panel was a magnetic compass, and the needle was resting on 189 degrees, roughly due south. He smiled secretly now he had his cardinal directions. It was little enough by which to navigate in bushy terrain like this, but it was better than nothing.

Looking back outside, he saw a four-man squad guarding one of the six-and-a-half-ton trucks. It didn't look any different from any of the other trucks, but it was the only one being guarded. Obviously there was something of special interest in that particular vehicle. If he had a chance before he left the area, he would try to find out what it was. After all, if James Bond could do it in the movies, why couldn't he?

Just then the short, dark-haired guy in civilian clothes he had spotted at the command vehicle walked up to the guarded truck. After speaking with the sentries, he opened the canvas closing off the rear of the truck bed and climbed inside. Sullivan wasn't at an angle to see inside the interior of the vehicle and when he leaned out to try to get a better look, one of his guards snapped something at him in Afrikaans and swung a rifle muzzle in his direction. He obediently sat back inside the skimmer.

Things were looking up, though. At least he knew where he was now, more or less, and he had discovered something the Boers thought was worth guarding even in the middle of their own camp. All he needed now was to find a way to get away from his guards and he'd be back in business. Until then he would sit in the back of his skimmer like a good little prisoner. To pass the time, he would run through all the movies he could remember about prison-camp breaks.

Maybe he'd remember something he could put to good use in his current situation.

ROSEMONT'S JAW was locked. He was royally pissed and was having a difficult time staying frosty in front of his NCOs and officers as he tried to explain why they had been ordered to stand down. Immediately following the emergency recall signal, he had received orders from Benning to pull back and go into a purely defensive laager until further notice. When he had protested, saying he had a man down and probably captured by the Boers, he had been told that now that the white hostages had been freed the status of the entire operation was being reviewed.

"But that's Mick out there," Ashley protested. "We can't just leave him!"

"Christ on a fucking crutch!" Rosemont exploded. "I know who's been captured, Wells. Give me a fucking break!" He ran his hand over the back of his neck. "Jesus!"

Ashley wilted in the face of Rosemont's verbal barrage. She had seen him mad before, but never this mad, and somehow, seeing him so angry made him more attractive to her. It showed more of the man than the tightly controlled exterior she was used to seeing before, and in spite of herself, she liked what she saw.

Part of the enigma of Ashley Wells was that while she loathed any signs of weaknesses in a man, she always challenged his strengths. And when she challenged a man, the reaction she received determined how she would treat him in the future. In her past battles with Rosemont, his cold, controlled responses had infuriated her, driving her to the point of deliberate insubordination. This time, however, he had lost his tight control and showed that he was more than the military robot he appeared to be. Now she could finally back off and quit playing her game with him.

"Did the Old Man give you any idea how long this review is going to take, sir?" Stuart asked, trying to defuse his commander before he detonated.

Rosemont took a deep breath. "No—" he shook his head "—he didn't. He just told us to hold in place and await further orders. We can defend ourselves, of course, but we cannot take offensive actions." He paused and looked at Ashley. "We can't even recon them."

"Isn't there anything we can do, sir?" Ashley persisted.

"We can sure as hell keep the Bats over them," he replied. "I'm not about to let those people get away from me in the bush. The minute that I get the word releasing us, we're going to hit those bastards with everything we've got and, as soon as we get Mick back, I'm going to grind their asses into the dirt."

Ashley smiled. That was exactly what she had wanted to hear. "War! War! War!" she chanted softly.

The United States Expeditionary Force's official nickname was the Peacekeepers, but the men and women of the Force knew what their real job was: they waged war. They kept the peace; that was true. But the peace they kept was only a result of the war they had waged.

More voices joined in Ashley's chant and it grew in volume. No one made war on the Peacekeepers and lived to brag about it, absolutely no one. Apparently the Boers didn't know this yet. But they would soon learn that there were easier ways to commit suicide than to mess around with the United States Expeditionary Force.

In spite of himself, Rosemont felt a tight grin form on his face and he joined in the chant. "War! War!"

SULLIVAN HAD DOZED OFF while in the skimmer and was shaken awake by one of the Boer security men. Motioning with the muzzle of his LAR, the Boer indicated that he should get out of the vehicle. Careful not to make any sudden moves, Sullivan stepped out. "I say, old chap, where are you taking me?"

The Boer merely grunted and made a follow-me gesture, so Sullivan fell in and followed. The two Boers marched him over to a chow line set up under the trees, where he was given an Israeli-issue field ration pack and a hot cup of coffee. Taking his dinner over to a tree, Mick sat down and ate heartily. As long as they were going to feed him, things couldn't be all that bad. At least on this mission, he was having a chance to sample some of the local cuisine. USEF rations weren't bad, but they got old real quick.

He quickly finished his meal and drained the last of his coffee. One thing he could say about these guys was that they made a real decent cup of coffee. "I say, old man—" he looked up at the Boer standing over him and raised his cup "—do you mind if I have another cuppa?"

The guard grunted and led him back to the chow line, where he got a refill on the coffee and a chunk of fresh bread to wash down with it. Standing under the trees as he drank the coffee, he took a long, hard look around the encampment. Whatever these guys thought they were doing, they were sure as hell going about it in the right way. Everything he could see was as squared away as any Peacekeeper operation. The crew-served weapons were all dug in and well camouflaged. There was minimum movement at the positions, and everyone looked alert. Sooner or later the Peacekeepers were going to go up against these guys again, and it wasn't going to be a picnic.

Sullivan looked back down and concentrated on watching the coffee in his cup as he pretended not to notice the short, dark-haired man who had just walked up to get his dinner. The Boer accompanying him was wearing the pips of a captain on the epaulets of his clean camouflage uniform and had the bearings of a staff officer. Even in the exile Boer army, you could tell the staff rats from the real soldiers.

The dark-haired man and the Boer captain talked quietly as they ate. Even though they were speaking English, Sullivan couldn't catch too much of their conversation. But from what he could hear of the dark-haired man's end of it, he thought he had managed to place the accent.

Sullivan had been in the Middle East often enough to recognize the particular brand of accented English the man spoke. He'd have bet an entire month's pay and Class Six allowances that the dark-haired guy was an Israeli. The question was, what in the hell was an Israeli doing throwing in his lot with these exiles? He wasn't a military adviser, or he'd be wearing a uniform. Also he just didn't have the look of a professional soldier; he looked more like an academic or a scientist.

Then it clicked. There was a good chance that the guy was a weapons technician. Back in the good old days, the South Africans and Israelis had worked together clandestinely on several weapons development projects. They had even secretly built and tested small tactical nukes and the medium-range missile delivery system to go with them.

In the clean up following the conflict in 2004, the Israeli nukes had been scrapped along with those of their Arabic neighbors. No nukes had been found in South Africa, although there were those who claimed that only a small nuke could have destroyed the big De Beers diamond mine outside of Pretoria. While the use of a nuke there had never been proven, it was widely believed and, fearful of radiation, the black government had never tried to reopen that one mine.

If this guy was an Israeli weapons man, there was a distinct possibility that he was involved with forbidden nukes, and that meant that the guarded truck could be carrying some kind of nuclear missile system. He had no proof one way or the other, but the mere suspicion of nuclear weapons was more than enough to send the Peacekeepers into action. Now more than ever, he had to find a way to get the hell out of here and report back to the company.

16

In the Bush, August 15

Rosemont stared out onto the darkening African plain as he made his hourly status report on the comlink. Echo Company's defensive position was well clear of the Boers' night laager, but Rosemont still had his security well out, covering all the approaches to his camp. Back at the Malaika airstrip, Bravo Company had also pulled back into a tight defensive perimeter to wait out the stand down.

Until the powers that be turned them loose again, the Peacekeepers were completely chained down and the waiting was wearing on everyone. The pride they had felt at having successfully rescued the hostages had quickly faded. It had been replaced with a feeling of helplessness and anger, and they didn't like to feel that way.

The Peacekeepers weren't used to political maneuvering getting in the way of their operations. Usually, by the time they had been called into action, the political bitching and biting had failed again, and the military option was the only possible recourse. The problem this time was that the military option had been stopped short by unexpected political maneuvering.

During the forty years of their self-imposed exile, the Boers had slowly built up a great influence in the international community. Outright bribes and further promises to grant lucrative concessions in the diamond and gold trade once they were back in power had gained them powerful political allies. The Boers were calling in all their markers now, and these allies were now calling for the Peacekeepers to be withdrawn.

They were also calling for United Nations troops to be sent in, and none of the Peacekeepers was happy with that prospect. From hard experience they knew that if the UN took over, the situation would rapidly turn to shit and they would have to come back later and sort it out anyway.

It would be far easier if they just went ahead and settled this right here and now while they were on the ground and in position to do it. It made no sense to give the Boers more time to prepare better defenses. Or, even worse, to get into one of the cities where they would have to be dug out one building at a time. At least now the Boers were in the open where the Peacekeepers could easily get at them.

SULLIVAN HAD GONE to sleep immediately after he had finished his dinner. His plan was to wake in a few hours, rested and ready to try to make a break for it. From the extensive escape-and-evasion training he had undergone as a Peacekeeper recruit, he knew that his best chance to get away was tonight, before the adverse psychological effects of being taken prisoner began to play on his mind. Knowing Rosemont, he was sure that Echo Company would have the recon teams keeping an eye on the Boer laager. All he would have to do was break free, head west and he would be sure to run into them. But even if he didn't, they'd be sure to spot him. Either way he'd be home free.

It sounded simple enough, but there was still the small matter of several hard-eyed Boers packing LARs who were taking a personal interest in seeing that he stuck around. He would just have to wait and see how many were assigned to guard him during the night.

SINCE THEY WERE stood down, the Echo Company command group had built a small fire and were heating water for coffee. They had a good supply of readiheat ration coffee canisters, but fresh coffee always tasted better.

"If Mick was here," Jeb Stuart said, "he'd be giving us a lecture on the old Boer wars and telling us for the hundredth time that 'laager' is an old Boer word for a military camp. I miss that mouthy bastard."

"We'll get him back," Rosemont promised, holding out his canteen cup for a refill. "You have my word on that."

Ashley looked skeptical. "What if the UN eunuchs move in and we have to pull out and leave him?"

The Peacekeepers' nickname for the UN troops indicated their total disgust at the ineffectiveness of the international organization. All too many times they had been called in to clean up a situation that had only been made worse by UN meddling. The record clearly showed that if a military solution was necessary, the Peacekeepers were the ones who should apply it.

"We're not leaving anyone behind." Rosemont's face took on a wolfish grin. "If, however, we do get orders to pull out, certain of us will simply resign from the Force and take our separation right here in Africa." His grin broadened. "And a certain amount of the tools of our trade will just happen to get left behind at the same time."

"I'd like to be on the top of that resignation list, sir," Ashley said seriously.

Rosemont smiled openly at her. "I rather thought that you might, Ash," he said, his voice warm and friendly. "Consider it done."

Ashley was shocked at Rosemont's words, but she was also secretly pleased. This was the first time he had ever called her by her first name, and he had even used the diminutive at that. Obviously he was no longer mad at her.

"Bold Lancer," the voice of the Bat controller back at the airstrip broke in over Rosemont's earphones. "Bat Charlie. I'm picking up a large force moving in on the Boer camp from the southwest."

"Who are they?"

"We think they're Simbas, Lancer."

"Affirm. What's their ETA?"

"Bat Charlie. I'd say that they'll be in attack positions within the hour."

Rosemont thought fast. There was no way he could warn the Boers and, even if he could, he wouldn't. The only problem was that if a full-scale firefight broke out in the Boer laager, it might endanger Sullivan. But it also might give him a chance to break away from his captors.

"Ash," he called out softly.

"Yes, sir."

"How'd you like to disobey orders and put your ass on the line for good ol' Mick?"

"Just name it, Major."

"There's a large Simba force moving in on the Boers, and I think there's going to be a major pissing contest over there in short order. If that happens, our man Mick just might take advantage of the confusion and try to make a break for it. And if he does, I'd like to have someone out there to police him up and bring him home before he gets himself lost. I'd go myself, but someone is likely to miss me.

"But—" he smiled broadly "—I can always say that I sent you out to patrol our security zone and you strayed out of your sector."

"I understand, sir," she said. "I'll take Strider Alpha and a couple of the Zulus."

"That sounds about right," he said, "but I want you to take more than just a couple of the Zulus along with you. That way, if I'm ordered to recall you, they can remain behind and keep looking for him."

Ashley donned her helmet. "That's most affirm, sir."

GUIDED BY THE TERRAIN nav information relayed by the Bat UAV cruising high over the Boer laager, Ashley and Kat's recon team ran through the scrub brush at a double time. Armed only with their spears and panga knives, six Zulu warriors ran right along beside them, easily keeping pace with the recon grunts.

According to the nav display, they were within a kilometer of the Boer camp when the faint rattle of automatic-weapons fire broke out from that direction. The first bursts were answered by several more, and in seconds a major firefight had broken out. This was exactly what Rosemont had predicted. "Pick it up," Ashley flashed to the recon grunts. "We've got to get in closer."

SULLIVAN WAS DRIFTING in a light sleep when he was awakened by the detonation of a large-caliber warhead on the perimeter of the laager. Instantly a storm of small-arms fire broke out on the southern and western sides of the Boer laager. Sitting up, he looked out the open rear ramp of the skimmer. When he saw that his guards were nowhere in sight, he dived out of the vehicle and rolled under it for cover.

Hiding under an armored vehicle full of fuel and ammunition in the middle of a firefight wasn't the brightest idea he'd ever had, but considering the circumstances, it wasn't exactly the worst, either. Until he figured out what was going on, he didn't need to take a stray round.

A flash of light from a near miss lit up the truck park and showed him the mysterious six and a half tonner that the Israeli had kept checking throughout the day. For once the truck's guards were not in evidence. As with his own guards, apparently the firefight had also sent them racing for their fighting positions out on the perimeter.

His curiosity overcoming his caution, he crawled out from underneath the skimmer and dashed over to the truck. The canvas covering the cargo compartment was lashed in place, and he fumbled with the ties. Ripping the last one open, he climbed up and dropped into the bed of the truck. The four objects lying in cradles in the truck's bed could only have been large-caliber artillery shells or missile warheads. Since he had seen no Boer tube artillery in the laager, they had to be warheads.

A flash of light from a detonation gave him enough light to clearly see what they were. The small yellow-and-black trefoil of the international symbol for radiation danger on the nose of the warhead closest to him blazed as if it were on fire. Instinctively he recoiled. A nuke! Sweet bleeding Jesus on the cross, the Boers had fucking nukes!

To anyone who had grown up in the Western world of the twenty-first century, the mere thought of a nuclear weapon was abhorrent. Only the most psychotic minds considered them to be anything other than the ultimate obscenity. But here they were right in front of him, four nuclear warheads.

He had no idea how powerful they were, but he knew that mere size was no determination of yield for a nuclear weapon. These could be small 1.5 kiloton tactical warheads, or they could be as powerful as the 20-kiloton bombs that had been detonated over Hiroshima and Nagasaki. Either way they were an obscenity.

Looking closer, he tried to read the stenciling on their sides. The language was Afrikaans, but he thought he could read one of the words: "neutron." It didn't mean much to him, but he knew that his brain would remember the words under chemical interrogation when he got back. It was absolutely imperative now that he escape tonight and get this information back to Rosemont.

If there was anything that would instantly send the Peacekeepers into action, it was nukes.

He had just stepped down to the ground when he sensed motion behind him and spun around. The flash of an explosion showed a figure bringing his rifle up to fire. Mick wasn't the unarmed-combat expert that Kat Wallenska was, but he had collected enough bruises on the training ground with her to have picked up one or two of her tricks. The best of those was the side-pivot kick to the groin.

The Boer let out a grunt when Sullivan's boot connected with his crotch, and he went down to his knees. His rifle fell free when he cupped his hands protectively over his groin. Instantly recovering, Mick lashed out again. This time the toe of his boot slammed into the point of the man's jaw, snapping his head back and sending him over onto his back.

Sullivan leaped on him and, rolling him over onto his belly, straddled his back. Reaching down, he grabbed the Boer's right ear with his left hand while he slipped his right hand under his neck and grabbed his jaw. With his knee in the small of the man's back, he put all his strength into a strong, sharp upward twist to the right.

Even over the roar of the battle, the snap of the Boer's neck sounded loud in Sullivan's ears, and he glanced around to make sure no one else had heard it.

Dropping the Boer's face into the dirt, he snatched up the man's fallen LAR, cracked the bolt to make sure that a round was chambered and clicked the selector switch down to the 3-round burst mode. He quickly stripped the body of extra magazines and stuffed them into the side pockets of his chameleon field pants.

He was picking up the Boer's legs to drag the corpse under the truck when he heard shouts close to the front of the vehicle. It was time for him to get the hell out of here. Dropping the body, he ducked behind a tree to get his directions. Fortunately most of the firing seemed to be on the southern and eastern sides of the laager. That left the western route open, and that was the direction he thought he needed to go anyway.

Sliding from tree to tree, Sullivan made his way toward the Boer perimeter. Trying to break out in the middle of a firefight was both good and bad. It was bad because the perimeter was fully manned and everyone was on alert. But it was good because they were looking for people coming at them, not running away from them.

Breaking out proved to be simpler than he had even hoped it would be. Even though his chameleon suit was no longer working, the default camo pattern it reverted to when the power was cut was dark. He darted from tree to tree until he reached the rear of the Boer positions, then he dropped down and crawled. The roar of gunfire masked the sounds of his movement as he slithered on his belly.

He had a tense moment when he crawled between two fighting positions and the one on his right sent up a flare. He froze until the flare went out and was able to get away without being spotted.

NOW THAT HE WAS CLEAR of the Boer lines, Sullivan couldn't see a thing. The muzzle-flashes and explosions of the firefight had destroyed his night vision and, since the moon wasn't up yet, he had only the light of the stars to guide him. He dropped down beside a bush and peered intently into the night, waiting to see if his eyes would recover their visual purple that allowed him to see in the dark.

Within a few minutes his vision had cleared enough that he could make out the faint shapes of trees against the skyline. He still couldn't see much at ground level, but he couldn't waste any more time and moved out anyway. There was always a good chance that the Boers would discover that he was gone and come looking for him. And since they'd be wearing full-sensor helmets, he wouldn't stand a chance of getting away from them once he was spotted. He had to put as much distance behind him as he could—and as soon as he could.

Up ahead he saw a small rise in the ground and headed for it. Once he reached the other side, it would block the Boers' sensors and detectors. As soon as he reached the small hill, he paused for a moment to get his bearings.

Suddenly a blow to his back knocked the LAR out of his hand and sent him sprawling flat on his face. As he rolled over, a body dropped on top of him, pinning him to the ground. The point of the knife digging into the side of his neck kept him from struggling.

"It's about time you showed up, Mick," Ashley growled, pulling the knife away from his neck. "Where the hell've you been?"

"I missed you, too, sweetheart." Sullivan picked himself off the ground and retrieved his rifle. "Now, give me a kiss and let's get out of here."

"Smart ass."

“And,” he added, “as soon as we can stop, I need to borrow your comlink and talk to the major. Those guys back there have nukes.”

Ashley stopped dead in her tracks. “That isn’t funny, Mick. Tell me you’re shitting me.”

Sullivan dropped the grin. “I wish I was, Ash. Honest to God, they’ve got nukes. Four of them, I saw ’em.”

“Oh, Jesus,” she said softly.

17

The Boer Camp, August 16

Dov Merov answered the summons on his comlink that morning and found Jan Rikermann at his command vehicle. In the aftermath of the previous night's Simba attack, the Boers hadn't moved out of their laager. Even though Rikermann was certain that his escaped Peacekeeper prisoner had reported the location to his headquarters, the Boer leader wasn't inclined to even try to run. He had come back to his homeland to fight, and in his view it was as good a place to do it as any other.

"Dov," the Boer leader greeted him. "I have just received word that the Americans also have a company of their Peacekeeper heavy infantry on the ground." He paused for a moment. "Also I don't know if I will be able to prevent them from interfering with my plans too much longer."

Merov didn't like the sound of that. "What has happened, Jan?"

Rikermann's face was grim. "Our political support is wavering. Though the politicians took our money and vowed their support, they are cowards and I suspect that they won't support us much longer."

His voice rose as if he were a prophet addressing his flock. "Once more, Dov, we are on our own against the world. But this time we aren't completely helpless. We don't have to defend our women and children this time." He clenched his fist. "We can fight this time and fight we will."

He grasped Merov's shoulder and looked him full in the face. "I want you to power up the Toro fighting suits and get them ready for immediate action, Dov. When the Peacekeepers move against me, I want to be ready for them. I will pit my strength against theirs, face-to-face, and God will decide the outcome."

Powered fighting suit technology was considered restricted military information in both the United States and Europe. The Hulk suits were too potent to allow them to be in the hands of the less stable nations of the world. But, as is always the case with technological secrets, once the genie is out of the bottle, it is difficult to put him back in. That had been the case with nuclear weapons technology in the last half of the twentieth century and that was the case with powered fighting suit technology in the twenty-first.

An American company with good political connections had been able to secure a technology-transfer permit from the State Department to allow the Argentines to build powered suits to be used in their logging industry. These were to be simple suits, designed for heavy lifting rather than for speed and agility like the military suits. Another American company had secured a politically motivated contract to build a ceramal-tile manufacturing facility for the Argentine space program at the same time.

Powered logging suits armored with ceramal and equipped with the high-tech weapons the Argentines were famous for equaled heavy infantry powered fighting suits in anyone's language. But with political influence confusing the issue, no one had made the connection.

By Peacekeeper standards, the Argentine Toro suits were crude. They were larger than the Hulk powered suits and, like the bulls they were named for, they were slow and somewhat cumbersome. While not as fast or as agile as the Hulks, they carried better armor and mounted first-rate heavy weapons. When the Peacekeepers came this time, they would feel the bull's horns.

Rikermann had intended to use his Toro fighting suits to clean up pockets of Simba resistance after the neutron bombs had cleared out the population centers. But now that the Peacekeepers were involved and had a company of their heavy infantry on the ground, it was time for him to bring out his own heavies.

"I will get right on that," Merov answered. "I should be able to have all of them powered up in about two hours."

"See that you do," Rikermann answered. "I feel that the time left to us is short, very short."

He paused for a long moment. "As soon as the Toro suits are ready, I want you to prepare the missiles for launching. We are within range of Pretoria and Johannesburg now. No matter what else happens, the missiles must fly."

Now it was Merov's turn to pause. Nothing about this operation had gone as Rikermann had promised it would. There had been more local opposition than he had predicted, and no one had anticipated that the Peacekeepers would be involved. Merov had understood that his neutron warheads would be used against civilians, but he had been able to rationalize it because he had been promised that it would result in a new homeland for his people, as well as for the Boers.

Rikermann had also said that once the weapons had been detonated and the Boers had reoccupied Pretoria and Johannesburg, their political allies would be able to prevent international retaliation against them. Now, however, he wasn't so sure. If Rikermann himself was doubting his supporters, Merov couldn't help but have his own doubts, as well.

Rikermann accurately read the expression on the Israeli's face. "I am confident that we can win the battle against the Americans," he said soothingly. "But even if God hides his face from us and we die here, I want South Africa to be free again. If we fail, our sons and daughters can follow after us and claim their legacy. But to do that, the land must first be cleansed, the Kaffirs must die."

Merov allowed himself to be reassured. He had come this far with the Boers, and if there was any chance at all that Rikermann would succeed, he had to do his best. After all, more than a dozen members of his own family were among those Israelis waiting for their new promised land.

"I'll put both the suit techs and the missile launch team to work, Jan."

"I will be praying," Rikermann said.

BECAUSE of their massive size, the Boers' Toro suits had been broken down for cross-country shipment.

The suits came apart at the waist, separating the leg and lower-back sections from the arms, head and upper body. To assemble the suit, the lower section, which was in an assembly cradle, was placed on its feet. The upper section was then lowered into the cradle and locked on to the lower section. Fully assembled, the Toro suit was three and a half meters tall.

Once the Israeli powered suit techs had assembled the first suit, Dov quickly powered it up and made the systems check himself. Everything was in the green. He called out to the Toro operators who were helping the technicians assemble their suits, and one young Boer power suit infantryman came to claim his.

He quickly settled himself into the harness and secured the muscle sensors in place. Snapping the armored shell closed around himself, he lowered the helmet faceplate, hit the master switch and watched as the digital readings flashed on his faceplate screen. Satisfied that the suit was functioning, he took his first step.

Sensing the movement of his leg muscles through piezoelectric circuits, the suit multiplied that movement through servos and the suit's leg took a step. To the operator, he felt as if he had taken a normal step. He exerted no more effort to move the 1200-pound fighting suit than he would have used to move his 180-pound naked body. With a faint whine from the servo units, the Toro suit lumbered over to the ammunition carriers.

While the weapons techs worked on the second suit, the armament men quickly loaded up the weapons on the first Toro. As soon as the last round was stowed, the operator clenched his right fist, and a short-barrel

20 mm machine cannon smoothly swung away from its stowed location, aligning itself with his zero-degree position. A twitch of his right index finger would fire the weapon.

A spin-off technique borrowed from the Argentine space program involved adapting a remote grappling-arm control system to use with the 20 mm. This allowed the machine cannon to be solidly mounted to the suit so as to soak up the recoil from the heavy gun.

The suit's left-hand controls operated a multiple-barrel rocket launcher system mounted on the suit's left shoulder. This system fired both AP- and EHE-warhead guided projectiles, as well as a short-range 30 mm grenade launcher. This combination of firepower made the Toros the most heavily armed fighting suits in the world.

As soon as he was fully armed, the Toro lumbered out to the Boers' defensive perimeter to await his comrades. In under the two hours Merov had promised, all twelve of the Toros had been assembled, armed and powered up. As soon as the last one walked off to take up its position, the Israeli reluctantly went to supervise the assembly of his missiles.

EVEN THOUGH the Zulus had been accepted by the Peacekeepers, they kept to themselves in the laager. Rosemont and Sullivan found Ka Umkhonto talking with a group of his warriors. He held a carved walking stick in his hands as if it were a royal scepter. He saw the two Peacekeepers approach and broke off his conversation.

"I have serious news for you," Rosemont told the Zulu leader. "Lieutenant Sullivan has reported that the Boers have nuclear weapons with them."

Ka Umkhonto's dark face couldn't hide his emotions. "I see you, Major Rosemont, but I do not hear your words. You are certain of this thing?"

"It is true," Rosemont said. "The Boers have nuclear weapons. Lieutenant Sullivan saw them himself."

Sullivan nodded his confirmation.

"And," Rosemont added, "these aren't normal nuclear weapons—they are neutron bombs."

Ka Umkhonto frowned. "I know of nuclear weapons, but this I don't understand. What is a neutron bomb?"

"It isn't like the normal nukes that destroy with an explosion. This kind of nuke kills all higher life by deadly radiation. With this bomb, everything is killed, but the buildings remain unharmed."

"This is a hard thing to believe—" the Zulu leader looked away "—that any man would do this. To face one's enemies with spear or gun in hand and to kill them, this is understandable. But to want to use a weapon that kills everything in its path—women, children, animals and the very land itself—is difficult to understand. This is a great evil and it must be stopped."

He raised the carved walking stick high in the air. "There will be a great washing of the spears and this Son of the Spear will lead the amaZulu against this evil."

"A 'washing of the spears'?" Rosemont looked puzzled. "I don't understand."

"I do, Major," Sullivan broke in. "That's the traditional Zulu phrase for a battle, a big battle."

Ka Umkhonto's dark eyes looked off into the distance. "It has been a long time since the Zulu have washed their spears in blood."

He slipped his walking stick in through the side of his loin covering and took up his spear and shield from the ground beside him. "I am named 'Son of the Spear' because my father killed a man in a duel to win my mother in marriage. He was the only man of his generation to follow the old tradition and was honored for it. At my birth it was foretold that I would live to see the old ways return. It was also said that I would bring great honor to the Zulu."

He raised his spear and shield. "The old days are back now, and once again the Zulu will be a mighty people. The Son of the Spear will make this come to pass."

From his recon team's bivouac several meters away from the Zulus, Ironstone watched their leader speak. An image formed in his mind in which he was watching a Comanche war chief from a hundred and fifty years ago preparing his people for battle against the American pony soldiers. Ka Umkhonto had the same quiet dignity as the old chiefs, the same determination to lead his people against impossible odds and superior weaponry, knowing that even if they did somehow win, it would only be at a terrible cost.

He also knew that just as the Comanches had been the best light cavalry of the American plains, the Zulu were the premier light infantry of the South African veld. They would face the modern firepower of the Boers without flinching and they would die, but they wouldn't die alone. Courage and honor would give them the arms and armor they would need to face the Boers. He almost wished that he could trade in his chameleon suit and LAR for a spear and shield and fight with them.

"Major Rosemont, your Peacekeepers have proven to be worthy warriors." The Zulu leader glanced over at Kat in the recon bivouac. "Both your men and your women. I will be honored to have them fight at our side."

"We are honored, as well," Rosemont answered. "We still hope that we will not have to fight. But if it comes to battle, we are honored to have you at our side."

"You will have to fight them," Ka Umkhonto predicted. "I know these Boers and I know how they think. They are a stubborn people and they think that they have their God on their side. But this is Africa and their God has little power here. The spirits of the old Zulu dead will decide the fate of my people, not the Christian God."

Like any professional soldier, Rosemont hated to see religion combined with the battlefield. It was far too volatile a mix. But this time he knew that it was inevitable. The Boers believed that their God had given them sole domination over the land they called South Africa. It was a belief that had little reality in the Africa of the twenty-first century, but then religious beliefs always died hard. This was one belief that was going to require a little more killing before it was completely dead.

Throughout history religion had always fueled the funeral pyres for those who killed in the name of one particular god or the other. It was as senseless in the twenty-first century as it had been in all the years of man's bloody history that had preceded it. But unfortunately this battle would continue the unholy tradition.

"Get your people ready," Rosemont said. "As soon as I get the battle plan, I'll pass it on to you."

"We are ready now, Major Rosemont, and our battle plan is simple." The Zulu raised his spear over his head. "We will drive the Boers from our land and destroy their evil weapons for all time."

Rosemont had no arguments with that.

WHILE THE PEACEKEEPERS waited, the international community went into a tailspin. The fastest way to end the Boer threat would be to take them out with a massive long-range air or missile attack, but with that solution went the risk of accidentally detonating the nuclear warheads. Also, if the warheads were hit, even if they didn't go into nuclear detonation, there was a chance they would be damaged and scatter the nuclear material. Because of that danger, the decision had been made at the highest levels to take them out through ground action alone. There were dangers in that method, as well, but it was felt that it was the least of the possible evils.

It was, however, also the most expensive solution in terms of casualties, and far too many of those casualties would be Peacekeepers. But as Rosemont had told Browning, that was what they got paid for.

18

In the Brush, August 16

There was tension in the air at the Echo Company encampment as the grunts awaited their orders to move out. Though Echo Company had fought many hostiles in many lands, it had been years since the Peacekeepers had gone up against a nuclear-weapons-equipped opponent. A few of the unit's senior NCOs remembered the campaign in Pakistan back in 2010. But the troops who would move out this time had never had to face the specter of nuclear annihilation, as well as the normal dangers of ground combat.

Every man and woman in the company had done a review of personnel files and updated next-of-kin and survivor information in the unit data bank. The realities of the situation weren't lost on anyone. Many battlefield comrades had also signed their lump-sum death-benefit payments over to each other with the instructions that the money was to be used for a party when and if the survivors returned to Fort Benning.

The conversations were terse and the jokes were grim as the grunts checked over their weapons and equipment again and again. When that was done, they turned their attention to their personal appearance.

Like the ancient Spartans at Thermopylae, who had amazed their Persian opponents by taking the time to comb out their long hair before fighting their doomed battle, the Peacekeepers also wanted to look their best in front of their enemies.

John Ironstone turned his head from side to side to look in his small field mirror at the fresh war paint he had put on his face. Three broad, upward-slanting black stripes adorned each cheek. The stripes had been outlined with a thin red border, and three white four-pointed stars had been painted on each of them.

"You look like you're going to a fancy dress ball," Kat commented when she saw her teammate. The Ironman always wore war paint when he went into battle, but usually only plain black stripes without the additional adornment.

The Indian grinned. "I want to make sure they know who they're fucking with today."

Kat grinned back and turned her head to the left. Her short, dark hair had been cut even shorter, completely exposing her right ear. In her earlobe she was wearing her biggest bright silver skull instead of the small black tactical earring she usually wore in combat.

"As Mick Sullivan says," she said with a smile, "if you're going to be one, be a big red one."

Ironstone laughed. "I wonder where in the hell he picked that one up?"

"He said he got it from a movie."

"That figures."

Ashley had also cut her short blond hair. Though she usually wore her hair a little longer than most of the female grunts, today it was cropped as close to her head as any of the men's. Rosemont was shocked when he saw her approach the CP. He had still not gotten used to seeing a woman as beautiful as Ashley with virtually no hair. But he had to admit that it made her stand out from the crowd.

"Recon is ready to go, sir," she greeted him.

"I like your new coiffure." He grinned.

She ran her hand over the blond stubble and smiled. "I'm trying to make the centerfold in next month's *Infantry Digest.*"

Rosemont laughed. "You might have to show a little more cleavage, Ash, but you've got my vote."

She looked him up and down, a sly smile playing at the corners of her mouth. "Don't you wish, Major."

ALTHOUGH the Peacekeepers were prohibited from moving any closer to the Boer laager, the terms of the stand down had been relaxed enough to allow the Bravo Company Hulks to move up to join Rosemont's grunts. When the Bulls arrived, the grunts saw that they had also adorned themselves for the coming battle. Every one of the Hulk fighting suits had been artistically emblazoned with a dull brown bull's head on the front plates. The bull's head was down as if charging an enemy, his red-rimmed nostrils flared and breathing smoke, and the arching yellow horns were tipped with dripping red. Their normal individual tactical numbers had been rendered in white on the bull's forehead.

Rosemont met Jim Collins, the Bravo Company commander, at his CP. "Who's your artist, Jimbo?" he asked as he eyed the fierce motif on the Major's fighting suit.

Collins grinned through his armored faceplate. "You like my new tactical markings, do you?" he asked. "One of the kids down in my maintenance section is a wizard with an airbrush."

Collins locked the legs of the suit, opened the front plate and hit the harness release so he could step down to the ground. "I figured that if we have to die here, we'll do it with our colors flying. Screw the regulations about not compromising the fucking camouflage."

Rosemont grinned back—he knew the feeling. If there was anything he could do to tell the world that his grunts were putting their lives on the line to prevent a nuclear holocaust, he'd do it in a minute. If they were going to die, they should do it in style.

Collins reached into the side pocket of his trousers and pulled out a sealed envelope. "We've gone completely tactical secure," he said as he handed the envelope to Rosemont. "Force says no comlink chatter until we move out again. These are your attack orders."

Even though the comlink transmissions were scrambled tight beam, they could be intercepted and, if someone tried hard enough, unscrambled. Rosemont quickly ripped open the envelope and read through the hard copy. The mission it outlined was simple: Echo Company was to support Bravo Company's attack. Together they were to close with and destroy the enemy by fire and maneuver. It was the purest essence of ground combat, the basic job description of the infantry throughout history.

"It sounds about right to me," Rosemont said as he folded the hard copy and tucked it in his jacket pocket. "When do we move out?"

Collins shrugged. "They're working on getting approval right now. There's been another last-minute hang-up, but Force has ordered us on a five-minute alert."

"Christ!" Rosemont shook his head. "I'm so fucking tired of waiting, Jimbo. I want to get this shit over with."

"That's most affirm, Alex," the Hulk commander agreed. "But while we're waiting, you guys got any hot coffee? All we have are readi-heats."

Rosemont laughed. When the situation had turned to shit and there was nothing you could do about it, it was an age-old military tradition to have another cup of coffee. "Sure, we always have a hot pot of coffee going at Chez Rosemont. Tell your Bulls to line up."

"I knew I could count on you grunts to know how to live well."

"God knows we try."

HALF AN HOUR LATER, Echo Company's recon teams were leading the Peacekeeper advance through the bush toward the Boers. The Peacekeepers had been waiting so long that when the final orders came it was anticlimactic. The grunts and Hulks alike simply stood, donned their gear, grabbed their weapons and silently moved out. Everyone knew his or her job, and anything that needed to be talked about had already been said. They would talk again when this was over.

Stuart's Second Platoon followed the point recon teams, and Sullivan's grunts were spread out with Jim

Collins's Bravo Hulks. The heavies advanced in six teams of two Hulks and half a dozen grunts. Most of the Zulus were out front with the recon teams, but Ka Umkhonto and a dozen of his warriors went with the leading Hulk team. No one thought it strange to see Zulu warriors armed with assegais and cowhide shields running alongside the ultimate in twenty-first-century ground warfare, heavy infantrymen in powered fighting suits.

Even though an air attack had been ruled out, the Peacekeepers' aircraft, both manned and the UAVs, swarmed around the Boers' positions. Until the operation was concluded, they had to be kept under constant observation.

Gunner Thompson led the four armed OH-39 Bubble Tops of Talon Flight at bush-top level. Had they dropped any lower, the scrub brush would have scraped against the bottoms of the rocket pods hanging from their stub wings.

Every pilot knew that the Boers had the deadly Rapier ground-to-air missiles in their inventory, but they also knew that the Boers had nuclear weapons in their arsenal, as well. They were willing to risk certain death from the Rapiers for even the slightest chance to take out the nukes. Right now, however, they were holding back, waiting for the Bravo Company Bulls to make contact and start the deadly ballet that would be this battle.

Jim Collins scanned the tac screen in his Hulk suit. Like all the other Hulks, he was taclinked to the recon grunts and the Bat UAV flying recon low overhead. Every ninety seconds the Bat flashed a recon update, but not much useful information was coming through. The Boers apparently had rather sophisticated electronic countermeasures and were successfully masking their forces from aerial observation.

The recon teams had also seen little of importance, but Collins wasn't reassured. He could read terrain as well as the next man, and the area they were crossing was a prime battlefield. The scattered trees, scrub brush and shallow gullies offered plenty of cover and concealment, but it was still flat enough to give good fields of long-range fire. The Boers were not amateurs, and he was sure they had sized up the situation the same way. If he were the hostile commander, he'd sure as hell use this piece of ground to his advantage.

Suddenly a streak of fire rose from the bush over a kilometer to his left front. It was followed by a dirty black explosion high in the sky. The data link to the Bat dissolved into meaningless static. The opening shot had been fired, and the Boers had scored a hit. It had been a hit to his "eyes," which could be the signal for the attack. Since this wasn't good terrain to be blind in, he needed to get some more eyes out in front of him ASAP.

Collins keyed his mike to call for one of the Bubble Tops to make a fast pass across his axis of advance when the Strider Bravo recon team leader broke in over his comlink.

"Dusty Lightning, Strider Bravo." The sergeant's voice was shrill. "They've got fighting suits! They're huge and they're carrying some kind of cannon!"

"Lightning, affirm. Flash it to me!"

Collins's tac display lit up with the data relayed from Strider Bravo. Strider was one hundred percent right. They were bigger than the Hulks and they were carrying some kind of heavy armament.

The Hulk commander's heart raced as the adrenaline flooded his system. He had been a heavy infantryman for a dozen years, and this was the first time that he had ever faced hostiles in powered fighting suits. On Peacekeeper operations, the Hulks were usually sent against armored vehicles because few nations had the capability to build the sophisticated fighting suits. This would be a first for the Bravo Bulls, and he was looking forward to it.

"Strider Bravo, Lightning," he called back to the recon team. "Good work, I have 'em. You'd better get your people out of there ASAP. The Bulls are coming and we're going to shake the earth."

"Strider Bravo, affirm. We're moving out now."

Collins switched over to his company frequency. "All Lightning elements, this is Dusty Lightning. We've got at least a dozen hostile fighting suits in sector three delta. They're big bastards, and it looks like they're packing some heavy firepower. Go to Red Team formation, I say again, Red Team. Keep an eye out for the recon grunts, but let's get in there and take these guys out."

A chorus of "affirms" answered him as the Bravo Bulls rushed into battle.

JIM COLLINS LED the assault on the hostile heavies. Red Team tactics grouped three Hulks together in a heavy-fire team, and was most often used against tanks or heavy bunkers. Since these guys were so damned big, maybe it would work on them, as well. From what he could see, the hostiles were moving in two waves about five hundred meters apart. But they were operating singly and without light infantry support, and that should make the Bull's task easier.

Thompson's Talon Flight Bubble Tops had joined in the assault. Flying in line formation, two of them swooped down on the lead Toro. Before the first gunship could fire, one of the Toros in the second wave raised his rocket launcher and fired. A Rapier missile streaked through the air, its vectoring nozzle sending it after the evading gunship. A fiery explosion in the air, followed by a rain of flaming debris, marked the death of the Bubble Top.

"Talon Lead," Collins called up to the gunships. "This is Lightning. As long as they've got those Rapiers, you guys had better back off and let us handle this."

"Affirm, Lightning," Thompson replied. "We've got to keep low until you can get them sorted out for us. If you can break 'em up, we can try to get in and nail the stragglers."

"Lightning, that's affirm. We'll call you when we can use you."

Using the Hulk suit's speed and agility, Collins's Red Team ran from one clump of brush to the next as they closed in on the hostile suits at twenty-five miles per hour. Tracking an interception course to the lead Toro on his tac display, Collins ran on ahead. His teammates flanked him in a V-formation as they followed.

Ahead, Strider Bravo had found a gully to hide in, but when they saw the lead Toro cross their front, they couldn't resist trying their luck. The two grenadiers on the team lined up the lumbering hostile powered suit in their sights and launched EHE grenades at it. There was only the faintest chance that they could disable it at the range they were firing, but it was worth a try.

One of the 30 mm grenades hit in the scrub brush, its detonation setting the dry vegetation afire. The second grenade hit low on the Toro's front plate and detonated. The Toro paused as if to check for damage, and the grunts fired again. This time the Toro leaped toward them, its short-barreled 20 mm blazing fire at the recon team's position.

Closing in, Collins saw the Toro go for the grunts. Swinging his M-18 Heavy Infantry Rifle around to bear, he fired a long burst on full-auto. The other two Hulks of Collins's Red Team immediately opened up on the hostile suit from both sides, as well. The Toro's front plate sparkled as the 8 mm fire bounced off the thick ceramal armor. Even firing AP rounds, the HIRs couldn't make a dent in the Toro.

The Toro turned away from the grunts to deal with the Red Team. Racing in closer, Collins fired a 30 mm grenade at almost point-blank range. He aimed for the Toro's gun arm, hoping to disable the weapon. The grenade exploded harmlessly, and the Toro's machine cannon barked flame in return.

The 20 mm AP/EHE rounds tore into Collins's Hulk suit, penetrating its ceramal armor before exploding. He felt pain in his chest and lower body, and his leg servos failed as he went down to his knees. Another blow to his upper body overpowered the gyros and sent him crashing over onto his back. When he tried to right himself, he felt only the pain from shattered limbs and torn muscles. The suit was powerless. His bio readouts were screaming in his ears, and he bit down against the pain as his fingers punched in the suit-destruct code.

He felt the explosive bolts fire to open the front plate and he took a deep breath of fresh air. The last thing he saw before his vision faded was the blue African sky. It was exactly the color of the infantry blue guidons the Peacekeeper companies marched under.

19

In the Bush, August 16

Rosemont was taclinked to the Hulk commander and saw Collins's bio readout blink red for a long moment before it faded from his screen. The thought flashed through his mind that he was glad he'd had a fresh pot of coffee going when the Hulk commander had stopped by. A man needed a good cup of coffee before he died.

As Rosemont watched, a Hulk from a second Red Team went down under the concentrated blast of a Toro's machine cannon. The other two Hulks in the team returned fire with both 8 mm HIRs and 30 mm grenade launchers, but their weapons seemed to have no effect on the bigger Toro suit. Rather than commit certain suicide, the team's survivors backed off, still firing on full-auto.

So far, the hostile fighting suits were ignoring his grunts and concentrating on the Bravo Hulks. But he knew that as soon as the Bulls had been taken out, the Boers would start in on his people. Against this kind of opponent, his grunts were doomed. They were as impotent as the Simbas at the airfield had been when they had tried to face the Hulks onslaught. The tables were turned now, and the only way he could keep from losing his entire command was to withdraw while he still could.

Force Headquarters was going to have to send in more than two companies to handle these people. But by the time heavier forces could be flown in, it would be too late. The Boers hadn't brought those nuke missiles along just to look at them. The missiles would fly and the damage would be done. As slim as it was, the only chance to keep the missiles on the ground was his grunts.

With a last look at his tac display, Rosemont quickly made his decision. By tonight workmen would be chiseling the names of the Echo Company Peacekeepers into the black granite of the wall of honor back at Force Headquarters at Fort Benning, his own included. But it had to be done. As long as they could fight, they would. After all, this was what they got paid for.

He took a deep breath and keyed his implant. "All Bold Lancer elements, this is Bold Lancer. This is it, people, we stay here. Get in there and do what you can to shield the Hulks. If you can get past the hostiles, make for the center of their position. We have to stop those missiles. Good luck. Lancer, out."

Slapping a fresh 100-round magazine into the breech of his LAR, he thumbed the selector switch down to the full-auto position. He had always led his units from the front line, not the rear, and this time would be no exception. He couldn't survive if his grunts were going to die, but he hoped that Ashley would get out alive.

ASHLEY WAS with Kat's recon team when she saw a dozen spear-carrying Zulu warriors burst out of the bush and race for the Toro that had killed Collins. By the white cow's tails he was wearing on his arms and legs, she realized that the warrior leading the charge was the Zulu's leader, Ka Umkhonto.

The Boer suit operator detected the Zulus and swung around to face their charge, bringing his machine cannon around to bear on them. A burst of 20 mm cut one of them down, the heavy-caliber explosive rounds destroying his body. A second man went down from a shell splinter in his chest, but still they came on.

"Fire!" Ashley screamed to Kat's team over the comlink, the LAR in her hands blazing on full-auto fire. She knew full well that the 5 mm bullets would have absolutely no effect on the Toro's thick armor, but maybe she could divert the operator's attention from the spear-carrying warriors long enough that they could escape.

As the fire from the entire team converged on the Toro, the Boer swung around to take care of the bothersome grunts first. But before the operator could bring the machine cannon around to zero in on them, the rest of the Zulus were on top of him.

One Zulu stabbed the thick steel point of his assegai into the back of the fighting suit's left knee joint. Unlike the closed joints of the Peacekeepers' Hulk suits, the Toro suit's joints were exposed at the rear. The spear point cut through the hydraulic line to the knee-action servo, and the leg locked in the extended default position.

When the Toro took his next step, he stumbled, and immediately the Zulus threw their weight against him. With the suit's gyros fighting to keep him upright, the Boer tried to swing his cannon barrel around to bear on his attackers. But before he could, the massive fighting suit toppled over onto its back.

The Toro crashed to the ground, crushing the leg of a Zulu warrior who hadn't been able to jump clear in time. The others ignored their injured comrade and piled on top of the fighting suit. One of them straddled the hot barrel of the cannon, trying to hold it down with the weight of his body. The servo-assisted arm, designed for heavy lifting, easily shook him free.

Before the operator could bring the weapon to bear on his attackers, another warrior jammed the heavy blade of his assegai into the shell-extraction port of the weapon's breech. When the Boer triggered the cannon, it got off only one round before the empty shell case struck the spear blade and jammed halfway out of the breech. The operator recycled the breech action several times, trying to clear the jam, but with the empty cartridge case wedged in the feed path, the weapon couldn't chamber a new round.

Now that the Toro suit was impotent, the Zulus took their time killing it. Assegais and panga knives sawed at the joints and the exposed servos. One by one the arms and the remaining good leg fell limp.

Ka Umkhonto repeatedly jabbed the point of his spear against the edge of the suit's lexan faceplate. Finally the spear point pierced the seal between the tough plastic and the surrounding ceramal armor. Prying upward with all his might, the Zulu popped the lexan faceplate open, baring the operator's head.

The Boer's scream was cut short when a short jab sent the assegai plunging deep into his forehead. Ka Umkhonto pulled the spear free and shook it over his head. His cry of triumph rang clear over the roar of battle.

JAN RIKERMANN SMILED. He was watching the progress of his Toro suit heavy infantry as they tore through the American Hulks as if they were light infantry grunts. Before he'd had the Toro suits designed, he had managed to get a copy of the classified specifications for the Peacekeepers' Hulk suits. Studying them carefully, his engineers had learned all the suit's capabilities and its few weaknesses.

Using this information, the Toro suits had been designed to go head-to-head with the Hulks and win every time. Not only were they more heavily armed, but also their armor had been specifically developed to withstand fire from the 8 mm rifles of the Peacekeeper heavy infantry. Once more, his careful planning was paying off. It was but one more sign that God had answered the Boer's prayers.

Therefore, Rikermann wasn't at all surprised that his Toros were tearing up the Americans, and he was supremely pleased. Once the much vaunted Peacekeepers had been destroyed and his missiles had been launched at their targets, he would be in a secure position to press his people's claims for the lands of South Africa.

Suddenly his tac screen showed that one of the Toro suits had gone down. The bio readout showed red, indicating that the operator had been killed. Rikermann was surprised, but he wasn't too concerned.

Though the Toro suits were good, they weren't invincible. He had expected to take some losses. Over the centuries the Boer people had shed much blood for South Africa, and a few more drops would make the land just that much more sacred.

ASHLEY COULD BARELY believe what she had just witnessed. Spear-carrying warriors had managed to disable and kill a twenty-first-century fighting machine that had beaten the best the Peacekeepers could throw against it.

She shouldn't have been surprised that it had taken the Zulus to show them how to deal with the Toros. The Peacekeepers were accustomed to fighting their battle in terms of firepower and the long-range kill, but the Zulus came from a tradition of hunting elephants with spears. To them, the Boer fighting suits were simply armed elephants with a bad attitude.

Killing the Toro suit had cost the Zulus two warriors dead and a third with a badly crushed leg, but they had done it. And if they could kill a Toro with little more than their bare hands, the grunts could do it too.

A second group of Zulus went racing up to another lumbering Toro suit. Quickly flashing orders to the team, Ashley quickly took it under fire, too. Again the Toro turned to deal with the grunts first. Like the Peacekeepers, the Boer operator considered the grunts armed with modern firepower more dangerous than the spear-carrying natives.

When the Toro turned his back on the Zulus, they attacked. As they had done before, they first disabled one of its knee joints and then toppled it over. This

Toro managed to kill only one Zulu before the spears bathed in the blood of the Boer operator inside.

ROSEMONT SAW what Ashley was doing and flashed it to Sullivan and Stuart. The two platoon leaders quickly issued orders for their grunts to break up into two-squad hunter-killer teams. One squad would attract a Toro's attention and once they were engaged, the other squad would swarm over it, disable its legs and then kill it.

It was an old military axiom that the best defense was a strong offense, and that was certainly the case this time. It was also axiomatic that ten little guys could always kick the shit out of one big guy. When combined with the cold, hard fact that no one lives forever, the grunts had found a winning combination.

The Bulls' XO, Lieutenant Tom Shaffer, saw what the grunts were trying to do and ordered the surviving Hulks to press their attacks anew. Trying to evade the Toros was only costing them blood, and if they were going to die, it was better to face them head-on the way the grunts were doing.

Collins would have liked that.

IRONSTONE HAD DETACHED himself from the rest of Kat's team and was stalking the Toros with his 8 mm SASR sniper rifle. During the stand down, he had been able to get the specialized weapon flown up to him with one of the ration runs to replace the scoped 5 mm LAR he normally used in the field. The heavier rifle packed quite a bit more punch, and he was anxious to try his luck with it.

He had seen the 8 mm fire from the Hulks' HIRs bounce off the Toro's front plates, but he had a better idea. As a sniper, he was used to searching out the enemy's vulnerabilities and carefully placing his shots where they would do the most damage. As awesome as the hostile fighting suits were, they had to have weak points and he would find them.

Snaking through the bush, the sniper spotted a small rock outcropping on the side of a low hill. He made for it and found a good firing position. Sliding in between two rounded boulders, he scanned his front for signs of the hostiles. According to his tac screen, he was on the left flank of the battle, but the scattering of hostile markers showed that several Toros were operating in the area.

Suddenly a Hulk appeared four hundred meters to his right front coming toward him at an angle. The Hulk seemed to have been hit, as it was having trouble staying upright and was only moving at a walk. Fifty meters behind the Hulk, a Toro burst out of a gully. The Boer fighting suit was moving in at a fast trot, closing in on the damaged Hulk for the kill.

As Ironstone quickly took up his firing position, the Toro fired a burst at the retreating Hulk. Ironstone saw one of the 20 mm rounds hit the Peacekeeper on the outside of the thigh, sending the Hulk staggering. It sank to its knees, unable to go farther.

Taking a deep breath, Ironstone focused his scope on the machine cannon on the Toro's right arm. When the cross hairs were centered on the 20 mm cannon's ammo feed link, he slowly released the air in his lungs and fired.

The 8 mm round hit the feed link where it went into the weapon's breech. The impact of the heavy slug drove the edge of the feed link into the nose of a 20 mm EHE round with enough force to detonate it. The resulting explosion set off several more rounds feeding into the breech and completely jammed the action.

From the jerky movements of the hostile suit's right arm, Ironstone knew that the operator was trying to clear the jam. He fired again, this time aiming at the Toro's faceplate. The round bounced off the armored plastic, and the Toro stopped trying to clear the jammed machine cannon. Even with its 20 mm out of action, the Toro wasn't defenseless. A multibarrel rocket launcher swung up from its stowed position as the suit's operator turned to face Ironstone.

The Indian threw open his faceplate as he brought his rifle up again. Even in the shadow of his helmet, the stripes on his cheeks showed plainly. Just as he had told Kat, he wanted these bastards to know who they were dealing with.

His next round hit harmlessly again. The Toro answered with a ground-attack rocket that didn't. The bunker-busting round hit the boulder Ironstone was crouched behind. The detonation of the shaped-charge warhead sent splinters of rock and shell fragments singing through the air. A red-hot, razor-sharp shard of steel sliced through the Kevlar thigh plate of Ironstone's chameleon suit, biting into his leg. Another frag punched deep into his gut.

Blinking the dust out of his eyes, Ironstone bit off the pain as he brought his rifle up again and focused the scope on the rocket launcher pod. He carefully chose one of the launch tubes that showed a warhead in the launch position. He couldn't tell what kind of a warhead it was through the scope, but if he could detonate it, maybe the rest of the rounds would go off, as well.

He squeezed the trigger, the rifle fired, and the Toro's left shoulder and head disappeared in a blinding flash. What was left of the suit staggered another half a step before toppling over onto what had been its face.

Dropping his rifle, Ironstone gave in to the pain of his wounds. His hands fumbled at the first-aid pack on the front of his assault harness. A quick shot of Neomorph, followed by a couple of stimtabs, and he'd be good as new. There were still more of those damned Toros out there, and he wanted to add another one to his trophy case.

When his fingers couldn't undo the catch for the first-aid pack, he lay back against the rock. He fumbled with his helmet and was able to pull it off. The sun felt good on his bare head. With the sky dominated by hostile antiaircraft missiles, there were no Dust-Off choppers standing by today monitoring the comlink bio readouts. If he was going to live, he had to do it for himself.

He tried the first-aid pouch again, and he was able to slip the catch this time. Reaching inside, he got the autoinjector of Neomorph but it fell from his hand.

He was reaching for it with his other hand when he heard a feminine voice by his head. "I've got it, grunt. You just take it easy now."

Through pain-filled eyes, he saw the face of an angel wearing the sweat-stained coveralls of a Hulk kneeling at his side. Her face was marked with blood and dirt, but she had the autoinjector in her hand and stabbed it against his good leg. The last thing he saw before his vision dimmed was the smile on her face.

"You got him, man," the fading voice said. "You really got the bastard."

The Boer Camp, August 16

When Rikermann saw the tactical beacons for his Toro fighting suits start blinking out one after the other, he panicked. Somehow the damned Americans were killing his Toros, and they had to be stopped. If they were destroyed, the remaining Peacekeeper Hulks would surely overwhelm the laager. Frantically he ordered his light infantry into the battle to support his remaining powered fighting suits.

Had the Boer leader had a stronger military background, he would have known the risks of sending armored vehicles alone against infantry in this kind of terrain. The Germans had learned the lesson with their heavy Tiger tanks in Russia, and Rikermann was learning it with his Toros now.

Like so many military amateurs, Rikermann believed that because the Toros were so heavily armed and armored, they were invincible. He had forgotten that the most dangerous thing on any battlefield is a pissed-off infantryman. The more pissed off he was, the more dangerous. And the Peacekeepers were pissed.

As soon as his orders had been acknowledged, he left the conduct of the battle to his operations staff. The battle was in the hands of God now, but there was still one thing he could do himself. He hurried to the center of his encampment, where Merov was pre-flighting the missiles.

He meant what he had told the Israeli. Even if his army was defeated here today, the missiles could clear the way for those who would follow. He had to send the missiles on their way while there was still time.

AFTER THE DESTRUCTION of the second Toro, Ashley and the rest of Kat's team had joined up with Ka Umkhonto's Zulus and together they went after more of the powered suits. They were closing in on their third one when she saw the flash of a massive explosion to her left, in the direction Ironstone had gone. Checking her tac screen, she saw his locator beacon blinking yellow, indicating that he had been hit. She also saw a marker for a Hulk suit close to him. The suit was disabled, but the operator was unhurt.

She quickly flashed a casualty alert to the Hulk, giving Ironstone's location, and requested that he make the pickup. When an "affirm" was flashed back, she returned to hunting Toros.

ROSEMONT HAD JOINED UP with a squad of grunts from Sullivan's First Platoon and they were infiltrating past the second wave of Toros. Now that the Peacekeepers had regained the momentum of the attack, he wanted to reach their outer perimeter as quickly as he could. He hoped that he could break through and try to get to those missiles.

Suddenly Rosemont's tac screen flashed a warning of an approaching Toro. Ducking into a brush-lined gully, the grunts pressed themselves against the bank, their weapons ready. The Toro operator was rushing to the aid of one of his comrades and passed the Peacekeepers without noticing them.

Raising his head above the bank, Rosemont scanned the area before giving the order to move out again. A flash of movement through the bush caught his eye. Scanning closer, his imager showed twenty Boer infantrymen racing through the bush toward him to join up with their heavies. If the Boers kept to their route, they would pass less than a hundred meters in front of the Peacekeepers' muzzles. Rather than hold tight and let them pass by, Rosemont decided to take them out.

"Okay," Rosemont growled as he ducked back down and warned the grunts. "Let's zero these fuckers."

The grunts quickly spread along the rim of the gully and readied themselves for the ambush. Though they were outnumbered three to one, they had their position going for them, as well as the element of surprise. The Boers were running full out to try to catch up with the Toro and wouldn't be watching their flanks.

Rosemont waited until the point man was only twenty meters away before he fired, dropping the man with a 3-round burst in the chest. His round was instantly joined by hundreds more as the grunts opened up on the unsuspecting Boers. Several of them went down in the opening volley before they could go to ground and seek cover.

The Boers were good and they responded professionally to the Peacekeepers' ambush. They quickly put out a heavy volume of counterambush fire, but the grunts didn't back off. They were pissed. They had taken casualties today and wanted payback.

Leaping from his covered position in the gully, one of Sullivan's grunts charged the Boers, his LAR blazing. Two others jumped up a second later and followed him. One of them went down to Boer fire, but before the other two could reach the hostiles the remaining grunts were out of the gully and charging behind them.

It was crazy, but Rosemont jumped up, too, and followed after them. Sometimes the best thing to do in combat was what came naturally.

In seconds the Peacekeepers were on top of the Boers, their combined fire cutting them to pieces. When their magazines ran out, the grunts didn't even stop to reload. Though they had no bayonets, the ballistic nylon buttstocks of their rifles made good clubs. The ferocity of the assault was too much for the surviving Boers. The remaining few took to their feet and faded into the bush as fast as they could.

When the last of the Boers were down, Rosemont looked back along the way they had come and spotted an empty fighting position twenty meters in front of him. Looking deeper into the bush, he realized that the assault had taken them up to the outer edge of the Boer perimeter. Several hundred meters beyond lay the wooded area in the center of the Boer laager. And somewhere in there were the nuclear-tipped missiles.

Bringing up the map display on his tac screen, Rosemont keyed his mike implant. "All Lancer and

Lightning elements, this is Bold Lancer. I've found a way through the perimeter. Disengage immediately and make for this location ASAP."

A chorus of "affirms" came over his earphones, but Rosemont didn't wait for the reinforcements. Taking his two wounded with him, he moved his squad up and occupied the empty Boer fighting positions before the hostiles could reclaim them and close the gap.

The first to answer Rosemont's call were Ashley and Ka Umkhonto's Zulus, who had joined up with Kat's recon team. "The rest of First Platoon's right behind us," she panted, out of breath from the run through the bush.

"I can't wait for them," Rosemont said. "We've got to get in there ASAP."

Leaving the two wounded grunts behind to hold the opening for the others, Rosemont led his impromptu force into the Boer laager. Now was the time when he desperately needed a Bat overhead flashing him an aerial view of the Boer laager. Just beyond the perimeter the scrub brush thickened as it turned into the stand of trees. His vision was limited to a dozen meters at the most, and he had no idea where the missiles were hiding. The same brush that was hiding the missiles could also be hiding more of the Boers.

Fuck it, they had come this far and it had to be done. "Follow me," he said.

BACK UNDER THE TREES in the center of the Boer laager, Dov Merov continued to prepare his missiles for launching. The launching stands had been set up in the open spaces between the trees, and three of the four missiles had been erected on the launchers. A last-minute guidance system glitch had been discovered in the fourth missile, and it was still being sorted out. Even if it wouldn't be functional in time, three neutron weapons delivered to their targets would be more than enough to do the job.

One warhead was targeted for Pretoria, one for Johannesburg and the third for the port city of Durban. The fourth had been intended as a backup anyway and wasn't essential to Rikermann's plan.

Merov wasn't plugged in to the tactical monitors at the launch site, but he didn't have to be to know that the battle wasn't going exactly as Rikermann had planned. As he had tried to tell the Boer, the Peacekeepers weren't the pushovers that the Simbas were. Rikermann had counted on the superiority of the Toro powered fighting suits to overpower the Americans. But from what Merov knew of the Peacekeepers, they would die in place before they turned back.

He tried not to think of the Americans as he halfheartedly attempted to trace the faulty circuit on the fourth missile. Finally he laid his tools down. What in the name of all that was good was he doing? He had already readied enough death to kill a million men, women and children, to say nothing of the animals and birds. How had he ever thought that his people could ever live in a land that he had wiped clean of life? Merov no longer believed in the God of the Jews, but he knew that if God did exist, he wouldn't want to see this land scoured by deadly neutron radiation.

He didn't really know what had caused his change of heart. Maybe it was because he was seeing the Americans risking their lives to stop Rikermann. Maybe it was because Rikermann had proven to have had feet of clay. Whatever it was, he had to undo what he had done. And he had precious little time to do it in.

Merov worked as fast as he could to disable the three missiles he had just preflighted and readied for launch. Standing the missiles down didn't take as long as it did to prepare them for flight, but it wasn't easy, either. The warhead circuits had to be disabled and the weapons made safe before he could deal with the rocket launch circuits themselves. One missile had already been shut down and the second one was almost completed.

He worked alone at his task. Now that the firing had gotten closer, his missile techs had all taken cover. Only the Boer security team remained behind, but they were in a tight perimeter around the launch site and couldn't see what he was doing.

He had just finished disarming the second missile when Rikermann raced into the clearing. The Boer ran directly to the launch console and slid into the seat. Switching over to the first missile, he energized the firing circuit. When the readouts showed multiple faults, he spun around to face the Israeli. "Dov, what have you done?"

"I couldn't let you do it," Merov said. "We're finished here, Jan. The Peacekeepers have won, and I don't want to go down in history as the man who nuked Pretoria."

"God won't let it be finished this way," Rikermann said as he selected the second missile. "We will take back what he gave to us."

Merov saw the Boer hesitate for a moment when the second missile readouts showed that it, too, would not fly. He glanced over at the Israeli, his eyes cold, before returning to the console.

"No, Jan!" Merov shouted when he saw the Boer select the firing circuit for the remaining missile—the one he hadn't been able to shut down yet. "Don't do it! It's over. We're finished here!"

Rikermann ignored him as he twisted the launch key.

Igniting with a roar, the nuclear-tipped missile lifted from its launching stand. Rising on a billowing plume of smoke and flame, it slowly gained altitude as the guidance system took over and it inclined to the west toward Pretoria.

Merov's eyes fell on the Rapier antiaircraft missile launcher lying a few meters away on top of the missile-control power pack. He dashed over, snatched the launcher, threw it up to his shoulder and spun around to face the slow-climbing missile.

With the huge IR signature of the massive rocket motor, the Mach-2 missile should have no trouble locking on to its target. Aligning the cross hairs of the optical sight on the flare of the rocket exhaust, he squeezed the trigger to the first stop to activate the guidance system.

The IR-seeking warhead purged and went active in a millisecond, hunting for the hottest thing in its field of view. As soon as the high-pitched launch tone sounded in his earphones, Merov pulled the launch trigger all the way back to the stop.

The Rapier left its launcher with a whoosh. Ten meters out of the tube, the main motor ignited, accelerating the antiaircraft missile to twice the speed of sound. At the same time, its vectoring motor swiveled to guide it to an intercept course with its bigger cousin.

Rikermann spun around at the sound of the missile firing. "You traitor!" he screamed as he reached for the pistol in the holster at his waist. "You have destroyed us!"

Merov lowered the empty launcher and turned to face the Boer leader. There was nothing to be said. He had done what he'd had to do and he really didn't care what the Boer did next.

As Rikermann aimed his pistol, a huge, angry orange-and-red fireball suddenly formed high in the bright blue sky. The sound and shock wave of several tons of exploding rocket fuel rocked the ground a split second later.

When the sound of the explosion rolled over the battlefield, Boer and Peacekeeper alike stopped fighting for an instant and looked up. Rikermann looked up, too, to see his dreams die in the billowing fireball. And when he did, Merov took off at a dead run.

Rikermann fired two quick shots at the fleeing Israeli, but the shots went wild. Taking a two-handed stance, the Boer aimed carefully. The Israeli had betrayed him and had doomed them all. He had to pay for his crime. The shot took Merov high in the thigh, and he went down. Rikermann smiled as he started for him.

ONCE THEY HAD PASSED through the outer perimeter, Rosemont and his grunts encountered little resistance. With the remaining Hulks pressing their attack on the other sectors, every Boer who could use a weapon was facing them on the perimeter. They were approaching the grove of trees in the center of the Boer laager when the missile Rikermann launched left the ground with a deafening roar.

Diving for cover, they huddled on the ground as the missile rose higher into the air. The sound of the rocket's motor was too loud for them to hear the Rapier fire, but the destruction of the missile made them look up at the fireball hanging in the sky. Something or someone had destroyed the missile, but the danger wasn't over yet. From Sullivan's report, there were three more.

Getting to his feet, Rosemont yelled for the grunts to follow him as he ran for the trees. Seconds later the suddenly roused Boer security team opened up from their positions inside the grove of trees.

Pinned down by the intense fire, Rosemont and his small force returned fire. He didn't know who had knocked the first missile from the air, but he couldn't count on the other missiles being destroyed that way. They had to break through and keep any more of them from being fired.

Laying down a base of fire, he sent Kat and one of her recon grunts around on the Boers' flank. Concentrating on the flanking maneuver, Rosemont didn't see Ka Umkhonto and his Zulus fade into the bush.

21

The Boer Laager, August 16

Shouting for his Zulus to follow him, Ka Umkhonto broke away from the pinned-down Peacekeepers and raced deeper into the trees. He had to get to the missiles before any more were launched. Autofire rounds cut through the brush after them, but most of them were directed at the Peacekeepers rather than the spear-carrying Zulus. Through the trees, he could see the two remaining missiles still on their launchers and he made for them as fast as he could.

Breaking into the clearing, he saw an older man in a tan safari suit with a pistol in his hand standing over a dark-haired man in civilian clothes. The civilian had been wounded. Blood showed on one thigh, and his right hand was pressed over another wound to his chest. Though he was injured, he faced the pistol aimed at his head without flinching.

The Zulu leader had never seen Rikermann before, but he knew who he was on sight. He didn't know who the other man was, but he didn't need to. The Boer was trying to kill him, and that made him a friend.

Though the assegai in his hand was a short stabbing spear, Ka Umkhonto threw it as if it were a javelin. The spearhead flashed as it sped through the air before taking Rikermann low in the rib cage, the tip of the point protruding from his back. The pistol dropped from his hand as he went down to his knees and fell over onto his back.

When Ka Umkhonto walked up to the Boer, his eyes were closed, but his chest still rose and fell with his labored breathing. Placing his foot on Rikermann's chest, he withdrew the spear.

A gout of bright red blood followed, and the Boer's eyes snapped open. "Kaffir!" he spit, the Afrikaans word for heathen. A froth of blood formed on his lips.

Ka Umkhonto stood over Rikermann, his spear poised in his hand. "Boer," the Zulu answered in Afrikaans. "Why do you want to kill the land you say you love?"

Rikermann coughed and spit blood. "We made this country what it is, Kaffir, not you."

"You are wrong, Boer." Ka Umkhonto raised his assegai again. "The God who made the both of us made this land, and we live on it only with his permission. No one has the right to kill the land. No one."

The spear flashed down, taking Rikermann in the heart.

As the Boer's feet kicked in the dust, Ashley and Rosemont burst into the clearing, their LARs leveled.

"Ka Umkhonto!" Rosemont called out. "Are you okay?"

"I am well," the Zulu answered, pulling his spear out of Rikermann's body.

He stabbed the spear point into the earth, wiping the blood from it. "We are all well now."

A WEEK LATER, the Echo Company grunts were drawn up in platoon ranks at the Malaika airstrip, standing at the position of parade rest. Though they were wearing their chameleon camouflage and were bearing arms, in place of their combat helmets they wore the proud green berets of the United States Expeditionary Force.

To their left the surviving Hulks of Bravo Company stood in their ranks. Unfilled gaps in their lines showed the losses they had taken in the battle. On the front plates of their powered suits, the Bulls proudly displayed the vivid bull's-head markings they had worn into battle that day. They would wear the distinctive markings from now on.

In the week since the battle, the last of the exile Boer strike force had been rounded up at their base in Mozambique and disarmed. Several ships flying Argentine flags had been stopped and boarded on the high seas, their cargoes of Boer troops and weapons being impounded. The Peacekeepers' Delta Company had made a capsule drop on the Boer headquarters in Argentina, taking hundreds of people into custody and shutting down their clandestine weapons facilities.

In Africa the Bantu People's Democracy had ceased to exist. Madame Jumal's government folded when word got out that she had been behind the assassination of President Bolothu. Accompanied by several Simba officers, she had fled, and an international manhunt was on for the fugitives. With her out of the way, an interim government had been formed from leaders of the late president's Centrist Party. Under the auspices of the Organization of African States, new national elections had been scheduled to be held in three months. Ka Umkhonto had already announced that he would run for president in that election and was expected to win.

Now that the military situation was well under control, the politicians and bureaucrats had surfaced again. A large delegation from the Organization of African States stood well off to one side of the Peacekeepers. A platoon of OAS troops wearing veld camouflage uniforms and red berets, but not bearing arms, stood in formation behind them. A smaller contingent of United Nations troops in their khaki uniforms and sky blue berets, but also not bearing arms, stood in formation next to them.

It was at the Peacekeepers insistence that the OAS and UN troops were not armed. Until they went home, they insisted on being the only armed force in the region. Although the remaining Simbas had been disarmed, they were taking no chances that some politician wouldn't see them as his way to grab power again. Once the Peacekeepers left, someone else would be responsible, but until then they were the Peacekeepers and they would keep the peace.

Facing the Peacekeepers, stood a hundred Zulu warriors in full ceremonial regalia. Every warrior carried a bright assegai in his right hand and a cowhide shield in his left. White cow's tails adorned their arms and legs, and many of them wore feathered headdresses. Ka Umkhonto stood in front of his men.

Rosemont stood out in front of his company's formation with Kat Wallenska standing one pace behind and to his left, bearing the infantry blue Echo Company guidon. Normally he hated this parade-ground bullshit. Unlike the Regular Army, the Peacekeepers were more concerned with the battlefield than the drill field. But Rosemont knew that this parade was more than warranted. His grunts had earned with their blood the honors they were about to receive.

When the United States Expeditionary Force commander, Colonel Bernard Jacobson, stepped out of the reviewing party, Rosemont snapped to attention, executed a smart about-face and commanded, "Echo Company! Ten-hut!"

As the grunts snapped to rigid positions of attention, their company commander faced about again. The colonel stepped up to Rosemont, and the officers exchanged salutes. Kat snapped the company guidon down to waist height, and the colonel fixed a battle streamer to the top of the pole. Kat snapped the guidon back up to the position of attention, and the colonel saluted it.

After another exchange of salutes with Rosemont, the colonel marched back to the reviewing party, and Ka Umkhonto walked over to the front of Echo Company. Like the rest of his men, the Zulu leader was in full regalia. Along with the white cow's tails and feathered headdress of the other Zulus, he wore a leopard-skin cape over his shoulders as a mark that he was of the Zulu royal family. A necklace of leopard teeth hung around his neck, and he bore the carved walking stick of his rank.

When the Zulu leader stopped in front of Rosemont, Kat snapped the guidon down again. Ka Umkhonto tied a twisted strip of leopard skin below the battle streamer, a mark of bravery. When Kat snapped the guidon back up, Ka Umkhonto called out in the Zulu language. A roar went up from the massed Zulu ranks as the warriors shouted their praise of the grunts and hammered the spears against their shields.

The Zulu leader then called out in English. "Major Alexander Rosemont, step before the Son of the Spear."

Rosemont took a step forward.

"Lieutenant Ashley Wells," Ka Umkhonto called out again. "Step before the Son of the Spear."

Ashley stepped out from her position in front of the recon platoon and marched to Rosemont's right side. She halted and faced the Zulu. Taking a leopard-skin headband from the inside of his cape, Ka Umkhonto placed it around the bottom of Rosemont's beret. He took a similar headband and presented it to Ashley. These were an honor given to warriors who had proven themselves in battle.

Ka Umkhonto stepped back a pace and shouted out again in Zulu. At his command, Zulu warriors stepped out from their ranks, each man carrying a small loop of leopard skin around the head of his assegai. The Zulus marched into the formation, each one stopping in front of one of the grunts. Taking the leopard-skin loops from the heads of their spears, they tied them around the right wrists of the Peacekeepers. When the Zulus turned to go, each man and woman of Echo Company now wore a leopard skin around his or her right wrist.

At Ka Umkhonto's command, the Zulu ranks again erupted with a roar and a drumming clatter as the warriors banged their spears against their cowhide shields. The cheering stopped abruptly at a wave of his hand.

"You are now Zulu warriors," Ka Umkhonto said in a parade-ground voice. "Wherever you travel in KwaZulu you will be welcome and will be shown honor for your bravery. The Son of the Spear has said it."

The Zulu leader then marched over to Bravo Company and presented the Hulks with the same honors.

AFTER THE CEREMONY, the Peacekeepers broke rank for a reception hosted by the OAS delegation. In view of the casualties the Peacekeepers had sustained in averting a major catastrophe, the OAS and UN were stumbling all over themselves to show that their efforts were appreciated. A lavish feed had been prepared for them with the finest bar in all of southern Africa.

After getting himself a drink and a bite to eat, Rosemont spotted Kat Wallenska standing off to the side and walked over to join her.

"Yo, Major," she greeted him, lifting her glass. "Great party."

"I just got the word on Ironstone," he told her. "He's going to keep the leg. It responded to the electrical stimulation and, with the growth-hormone therapy, he'll be back for duty in a couple of weeks."

Kat grinned. "That malf. He's just trying to skip out on the post-operation maintenance. He's probably found a new squeeze at the hospital and wants to spend the time patting her on the ass."

"As a matter of fact," Rosemont said with a smile, "he did say that he wanted to take a week off when he gets out of the hospital. Something about wanting to thank the female Hulk who patched him up that day."

Kat laughed. "Leave it to the Ironman to find a new squeeze in the middle of a battlefield.

"Speaking of time off," she asked boldly. "Where are you going on R and R this time?"

Rosemont paused. The thought of spending some more time with Kat was tempting, very tempting. Since she was a soldier, she understood him better than any woman he had even known and it was easy to talk to her. Also she had a way of keeping what happened on R and R behind when they had to go back to duty.

The invitation was tempting, but this time he had to refuse. Another soldier in his command had already asked for his company and he hadn't been able to turn her down.

"I'd like to," he said. "But I'm going to stick around Benning this time."

Kat looked over to where Ashley Wells was standing next to Lieutenant Sullivan. The slim blond platoon leader was talking to Mick, but her eyes kept flicking over to Rosemont. Kat had seen that look before and knew what it meant.

"No sweat, Major," Kat said with no trace of jealousy in her voice. It was about time that Ash learned how to wind down after an operation. "Maybe I'll catch you another time."

"Maybe, Kat," he replied.

"And, Alex?"

"Yes."

Kat smiled impishly. "Good luck."

"Thanks," Rosemont chuckled. "I may need it."